An Ext
Love *of*
Coffee

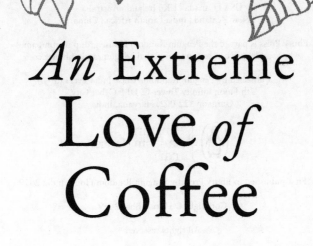

An Extreme
Love *of*
Coffee

HARISH BHAT

EBURY
PRESS

An imprint of Penguin Random House

EBURY PRESS

USA | Canada | UK | Ireland | Australia
New Zealand | India | South Africa | China

Ebury Press is part of the Penguin Random House group of companies
whose addresses can be found at global.penguinrandomhouse.com

Published by Penguin Random House India Pvt. Ltd
7th Floor, Infinity Tower C, DLF Cyber City,
Gurgaon 122 002, Haryana, India

First published in Ebury Press by Penguin Random House India 2019

10 9 8 7 6 5 4 3 2 1

This is a work of fiction. Names, characters, places and incidents are either the
product of the author's imagination or are used fictitiously and any resemblance
to any actual person, living or dead, events or locales is entirely coincidental.

ISBN 9780143449119

Typeset in Perpetua by Manipal Technologies Limited, Manipal
Printed at Manipal Technologies Limited, Manipal

www.penguin.co.in

To my parents,
who gifted me my first storybook over fifty years ago
and encouraged me to constantly read, write and explore

CONTENTS

PART A: A Coffee Adventure   1

PART B: The Search   87

PART C: The Final Clue   143

PART D: The Monk's Treasure   213

Afterword   241

Acknowledgements   243

A Note on the Author   245

PART A

A COFFEE ADVENTURE

1

When Rahul first developed an extreme love of coffee, he had not imagined even remotely where this affair would lead him. It had only been a year but this obsession had marked a sudden, clean and dramatic shift from his long-standing penchant for elaichi chai.

When his colleague Srinivasan, the accountant who sat in the cubicle next to his, commented on this change, Rahul was quick to respond, 'It is elaichi chai that I've been having since my college days. How long can one keep drinking the same thick, syrupy stuff? Coffee, on the other hand, is so seductive and cool, man. Good coffee is like delicious, lingering sex, you know?'

Srinivasan, a nearly celibate Tamil Brahmin from Trichy (also called Tiruchi or Tiruchirappalli), did not like these casual mentions of sex in the office. However, well aware that Rahul was in an expansive mood, one where he would go on and on about assorted and inane things, Srinivasan persevered with the conversation, probably for the sake of friendship. It was only when it became quite likely that more graphic descriptions would follow to further illustrate what was already an inappropriate comparison that he thought it best to walk back to his cubicle. Shaking his head, he buried himself in the safety of his accounting ledgers where coffee and lingering sex thankfully made no appearances.

Rahul Kamath, a man from the world of advertising and a newly converted lover of coffee, sat back in his chair. He brushed back his thick black hair, stared into space and then closed his eyes. This almost always helped him think. *Why did Srini go away so quickly?* Rahul could never understand people who first initiated a conversation and then withdrew inexplicably. *Unfortunately, there are plenty of such people in our offices these days—shallow guys with thick spectacles and a bucketload of grand degrees, most of them unable to hold a conversation for more than a few minutes. Let it go, let it go, Rahul, it is not worth the thought.* Only a nice hot cup of freshly brewed black coffee was worth his time now; some lovely Americano would allow him to think and rise above the usual rut that was office civility.

Rahul took off for the Starbucks café at Horniman Circle, his favourite coffee place. It was a delightful coffee house, cozy and warm, and just ten minutes away if one walked briskly. It had a buzz that fed his creative juices. But now, just the thought of a steaming cup of Americano had geared him up for some thinking. He had read somewhere that Americano literally meant American coffee though it had actually originated in Italy. This nugget of information had intrigued him until he found an unconfirmed story suggesting that the name owed itself to American soldiers fighting in Italy during World War II. They used hot water to dilute the strong Italian espresso to produce the sort of coffee they drank at home. The Italians must have been aghast. But he doubted if anyone cared; after all Americano helped the Americans win the war.

To reach Starbucks at Horniman Circle, one had to cross St Thomas Cathedral, a three hundred-year-old landmark of south Mumbai and one of the oldest churches in India. Rahul cast a glance at the cathedral, a bright yellow and white Gothic building that radiated cheer and peace. The intricately crafted ornate fountain at the entrance had always intrigued him. He also recalled seeing the beautiful stained glass windows inside the cathedral, which featured the apostle Saint Thomas with the Bible in one hand and a T-square in the other, showing everyone that he was a builder by profession. *What an interesting visual depiction*, he thought to himself. Then, he took a quick bend around the corner, saw the historic Horniman Circle right in front of him and reached the heritage building that housed the Starbucks café.

*

Even in the middle of the afternoon, Starbucks was abuzz with activity—people eating, drinking, reading and mostly talking. On that particular day, most of the men looked like they were aspiring artists, but Rahul knew this was purely conjecture based on their dishevelled clothes and banded ponytails. Three of the five women that he saw wore large silver earrings and pendants while the other two were without ornaments. There was also a strange-looking man he had never seen before, and the only vacant seat in the café faced him. Rahul had to make peace and sit there.

'Can I have a Caffè Americano?' he asked the young barista wearing a green apron. 'And please make it as strong as you can. I love strong coffee.'

'Absolutely!' replied the barista with a nod of approval. The black coffee was soon served to him, a generous serving in a huge porcelain mug. And then, as he took his first sip, unbelievable things began to happen.

2

Aren't unbelievable things too commonplace these days? Nothing surprises anyone any more.

Rahul was always sceptical of such things. *Nonsensical stuff, figments of imagination, even downright lies*, he thought. As the warm coffee streamed down his gut, he sat up thinking about his project. His boss, well-known advertising guru Haroon Sawant, had asked him to create a stunning film for an Ayurvedic herbal hair oil that served a single-minded purpose: using it before bed allowed for eight and a half hours of uninterrupted, deep sleep.

'Nidra Hair Oil needs your magic touch, Rahul,' Haroon had told him two weeks ago. 'How do we break through all this meaningless clutter and create a film that makes people long for this oil? People need to sleep, Rahul. Sometimes, they need to sleep with each other. Or they may voluntarily want to sleep alone, though that makes no sense really to a guy like me. To each his or her own sleep, of course. But I can tell you this, irrespective of how we sleep, we need lots of it, all eight and a half hours. What is a man without sleep? For that matter, what is a woman without sleep? Nidra is such an apt name too. Don't you think?'

For two weeks, Rahul had been working on the script. He had been trying, quite tenaciously in fact, but he had nothing to show for it. One useless script after another had found its way into the bin. All was consumed. There was evidence too—Gold Flake cigarettes, Kingfisher beer and Old Monk rum. Just no script.

And then it suddenly struck Rahul. He knew what the problem was. He knew why he couldn't think of a good film. Every good script he had ever written had started with the idea of his protagonist. In this case he would need to see who the model was, derive inspiration and write the story around her. This was his way.

Only this time, he had no idea who his muse was to be for Nidra oil. Amidst this general listless gloom, the first few sips of the black coffee somewhat brightened him. He looked up and was instantly taken aback, delightfully so. The odd-looking man in front of him had left and been silently replaced by two stunning women. They were drop-dead gorgeous. Rahul could smell the amalgam of their unique perfumes.

Interestingly, they wore identical sarees, leaf-green cottons with floral red patterns on the pallu. Both of them wore large gold nose rings, the kind that belonged to a different era, the sort no one wore any more. They also wore matching skin-coloured blouses. Rahul asked himself, *when did they walk in? What were they doing here, and why had they occupied his table? Who were they?*

Before Rahul could reflect on this sudden flush of questions, one of them fluttered her thick eyelashes and spoke, 'Hi, Rahul. I am Urvashi and this here is my friend, Heena. Like you, we love our coffees. I like mild, freshly brewed arabica coffee. Heena likes a mean double shot of espresso. Stop looking around uselessly and look at our hair instead.'

The barista suddenly reappeared and handed over a white coffee mug to Urvashi and a small brown espresso cup to Heena. 'Here you go, dearies, your regular fixes.' She then turned to Rahul and smiled. 'Don't worry about these girls. They are nice and talkative, but if you really want space they will leave you alone. I know them well.'

'Look at our hair, Rahul. Look, look, look,' Heena was speaking now, running her hand through her tresses.

Rahul stared at their hair. Lush, dark tresses of jet-black hair falling past their shoulders and blouses, all the way down to their little feet that were partly hidden under the table. He looked up and down all the way a couple of times.

'Do you girls sleep well at night?' he asked. God alone knew what came over him and compelled him to ask this. It must have been the frustration of not being able to finish his project.

Urvashi said, 'Yes, of course we did, Rahul. We sleep very well. Always.'

He thought he spotted a hint of a thin smile curled on her thick lips. *How did they know my name? I am an anonymous twenty-eight-year-old trying to make it somewhere in life. I am no Haroon Sawant.*

'We sleep for eight and a half hours each night. Warm deep sleep; curled up in the trusses of our well-oiled hair. That's what keeps us so bright and chirpy. We need our long hours of sleep, Heena, don't we?' With this, they broke into an endless stream of laughter. Then the laugh transformed. It became lighter, happier, almost bordering on flirtatious.

Right then, Rahul knew that he had found his models for the Nidra oil film—Urvashi and Heena—beautiful, long-haired women who slept for eight and a half hours every night. So perfectly authentic that it could be mistaken for a set-up.

'But let's speak about coffee now, Rahul. That's why we are here, you know,' Urvashi continued, cupping her mug in both hands. 'This is my favourite brew; deep and earthy flavours. I can feel the notes of mild orange running down my tongue. There is that little hint of lemon too. You know, Rahul, I love citrus flavours in my coffee. This coffee must be from Coorg. Lightly roasted arabica, I guess. What joy!'

Rahul sipped on his coffee and recognized the orange and citrus flavours too. It tasted marvellous. If only he had discovered coffee a few years earlier. Instead of all those thick, milky elaichi chais and saccharine-infested diet colas, he could have enjoyed many thousands more warm cups of coffees by now. Suddenly, Rahul snapped back to his senses. These gorgeous women and their graphic descriptions of coffee didn't seem to make any sense whatsoever. *Why were they here?*

He closed his eyes. He always did this when he wanted to focus and think. Sometimes, like now, he pressed his eyelids together even deeper and ran his hands over his eyes; it helped him think better. When he opened his eyes, they were gone, out of sight. Shortly after, Starbucks announced that it was closing for the afternoon. The barista thanked him with a smile and bid him goodbye

3

That night, sitting before his computer at his small, round dining table, Rahul typed out his script for the Nidra oil film. In one hour of frenzied, inspired writing, he had the entire story ready, down to every little scene.

INT. LIVING ROOM—NIGHT

MENEKA: Early twenties, glowing, fit, with thin hips, thick lips and shapely breasts, walks disheartened into her Lokhandwala living room (small and cramped, but chirpy and colourful). Her roommate, Saira (same physical features, but with curly hair), switches the TV off and approaches her. They both have dark circles under their eyes due to lack of sleep—not uncommon in Mumbai.

SAIRA (sadly approaching Meneka): Tujhe bhi call mila [Did you get a call too]?

MENEKA: Haan. Lekin kal 7 baje ABC studios jaana hai. Itna jaldi uthi toh director ko mein nahin, mere dark circles dikhenge! (points at her under-eye bags. Saira shakes her head and then smiles.) [Yes. But I have to be there at 7 a.m. If I wake up so early, the director will only notice my dark circles, not me]

SAIRA: Pagli! Solution mere paas hai! [Don't be crazy. I have a solution]

Saira brings out a bottle of NIDRA HAIR OIL. She points it towards the screen and then hands it to Meneka.

MENEKA: Nidra Hair Oil?

Saira smiles.

CUT TO: INT. BEDROOM—NIGHT

Now in their nightdresses (modern, short and translucent, the girls get ready for a good night's sleep. Saira slowly, and sensually, applies some NIDRA HAIR OIL (golden drops) on to Meneka's long hair that falls to her feet. The latter smiles as she catches a whiff of the pleasant odour. Meneka repeats the process on to Saira's hair. They cuddle for a while before falling asleep in each other's arms, surrounded by the warm scent of the oil.

As the two sleep, we move to an insert of a clock that reads 10 p.m.

LAPSE TO 6 a.m.

The girls are still asleep.

LAPSE TO 6.30 a.m.

Without any alarm, the girls get up. Meneka feels fresh as she extends her arms into the air. Her under-eye bags are gone, her hair feels silkier. Saira, simultaneously, extends her hands forward. They hold hands softly, for just a moment.

INT. BATHROOM—EARLY MORNING

Meneka checks her eyes and finds no dark circles.

BLUR OUT.

A small on-screen product placement with narration. A young feminine voice takes over.

FEMALE NARRATOR (V.O.)

Nidra Hair Oil. Silky hair and eight and a half hours of sleep. Guaranteed, with the science of Ayurveda.

Rahul was particularly happy that he had featured two women in his story. There were clear homosexual overtones to this film, though everything was to be done tastefully without the slightest suggestion of anything semi-sexual, delicious or lingering or otherwise. He was sure the film would work because he had once read that seeing two women together in bed turned on both men and women. Everyone would want to see this story again and

13

again, and then hopefully they would buy gallons and gallons of the wretched oil.

Rahul was certain that Haroon too would love the story because of its unique angle. He hoped it would be seen as a pioneering, liberating and progressive move in the world of Indian advertising. Maybe even an award at Goa or Cannes. Who knew?

Both Haroon and Ram Kishan Gupta, the marketing head of Nidra Hail Oil, loved the film. Haroon even gently patted Rahul on the back in a rare gesture of appreciation. When they looked around for the right actresses to cast in the film, a number of names and photographs came up as suggestions from various model coordinators.

Rahul turned over these photographs and, suddenly, there they were. Honestly, even before he saw them, he was half-expecting them—Urvashi and Heena—to be there. Their names were tagged in a big, bold font. 'Urvashi Mehta. Twenty-eight years. TV actress and model. Speaks Hindi and Gujarati fluently and a little bit of Marathi.' And then there was Heena Begum. 'Thirty years. Model. One small acting appearance in a Salman Khan movie. Speaks Hyderabadi Hindi, Urdu and Telugu.' Both the pictures featured thick lips, sparkling eyes, sultry smiles, big gold nose rings, exactly how he remembered them from the Starbucks café at Horniman Circle. They were the perfect cast.

*

The Nidra advertisement delivered superbly. Everyone loved it. Social media went to town calling it one of the biggest creative ideas of the year. The *Advertising Weekly* wrote: 'Why on earth had no one thought of this earlier? Casting two beautiful women together to advertise a product that clearly has its origins in gorgeous feminine hair is just the most natural thing to do. Rahul Kamath has started something new here, and we must rise and applaud him.'

The *Bombay Marketing Journal* was even more effusive in its praise. 'Nidra Hair Oil is lifted into ethereal heights by this fantastic piece of advertising. It is sensuous and poetic at the same time, and the casting is perfect. Where were both these women hiding before they appeared in this advertisement with their long hair and deep eyes? How did Rahul Kamath have the courage to cast them together in the bedroom, something no advertising film-maker has ever done before? Here is poetry and hair oil blended together perfectly. Take a bow, Rahul.'

Ram Kishan Gupta was more matter of fact but equally positive. 'Nidra Hair Oil has grown by an amazing 38 per cent over the past few months, making us the undisputed market leader in the sleep-well segment. With such fantastic growth, we are well on our way to providing many more millions of Indians their richly deserved eight and a half hours of sound sleep. A significant contributor to our success and growth has been the brilliant advertisement campaign crafted by Rahul Kamath, under the most able guidance of the one and only Haroon Sawant. Nidra looks forward to continued strong partnership with this creative and committed duo.'

Such praise meant limelight and more business. Haroon was particularly excited by a phone call he received from Ram Prakash, the founder of Nippon Springlove, an upcoming mattress manufacturer from Mysore.

'Help me take Nippon Springlove to every Indian bedroom, Haroon. Do for me exactly what you did for Nidra Hair Oil. We have great mattresses backed by patented spring technology from Japan, the sort that helps you perform like a dream, sleep like a dream and have a flexible back like a dream. I have the exclusive licence for this technology from Yamamato himself, a specialist in bed springs. He has a cult following in Japan. But no one knows about us in India,' he said wistfully.

After a pause, he added, 'If there's anyone who can do this for us, it is you and Rahul. We'll offer you not just a fixed fee but also a full 10 per cent of our sales revenues.' They set up a meeting for the following month. Meanwhile, Ram Prakash sent them two king-sized Nippon mattresses to try out, which both Haroon and Rahul agreed was a particularly nice touch.

Haroon was overwhelmed by all this and, in a rare moment of weakness, offered Rahul fifteen days of paid holiday as a reward. 'Spend your time on some mountain or beach, Rahul. Go deep into a forest if you wish to. The creative mind needs nature and space and beer and wine. Go!' Haroon didn't forget to mention, 'And while you are there, Rahul, think a little about an advertisement for Nippon Springlove. This deal can make us really rich, you know? Who in this tight-fisted world offers 10 per cent of his revenues? Imagine! 10 per cent!'

Rahul sat back and thought about all this, happily anticipating a paid vacation, an important question weighing on his mind: Where should he go for an entire fortnight? He was back at his favourite Starbucks café. He had in front of him a small, bright red cup of espresso. Espresso had always been his beverage for solitary, quiet moments of celebration. A small sip of the thick black coffee, almost the thickest he had ever tasted, and all his senses came to life. He could hear his deep, silent breaths, clear and suffused with rich espresso aroma. Coffee was magic.

No wonder the Italians loved their espresso—the coffee of the squeeze. It was the very essence of the bean, extracted within forty-five seconds under relentless pressure. Unlike human beings, coffee beans don't cave in to unabating stress. When pressed to perform, they give their very best. *What a nice idea! Definitely worth stowing away safely in memory for future use. Marketers and advertising film-makers should never throw ideas away.*

With his eyes shut, he savoured the viscous coffee, rolling it around just a little on his tongue. This time when he opened his eyes there were no long-haired, gorgeous women around. Instead, there was something else. On his table, next to his cup, was a small promotional brochure that someone from the café had placed there. It had pictures of ripe, red coffee berries and lush green plantations. Gorgeous bushes with broad leaves and trees with vines running up their trunks. He turned the pamphlet over to find elephants on the back, standing amidst the coffee bushes. There were a few interesting-looking birds with long multi-coloured beaks as well. What appealed to Rahul instantly was the presence of delicious and warm embrace of coffee everywhere. The brochure spoke about relaxing coffee holidays in Coorg, on the foothills of the Western Ghats, deep inside the home of Indian coffee.

4

'You want to go to Coorg for a holiday? Why Coorg of all places? Why not Turkey or Vietnam or Ladakh, or some cool place like that?' Neha's WhatsApp message had an inquiring tone, but Rahul could sense an undertone that was mildly, just mildly, complaining.

'Well, let me think, Neha,' Rahul typed back. He then followed that up with one of the most inspiring WhatsApp messages he would ever write. 'Because coffee nourishes my soul, Neha, and Coorg is where it grows. Because the ripe, red coffee cherries can ignite magic in our hearts and we will see them down there in abundance. Because freshly roasted coffee, sipped right at the plantations, is a rare and beautiful experience. I believe it is where you and I can find what we really want, in our own little cups.' As a final flourish, for good effect, he added, 'Let's have our coffee black as night, sweet as sin, in Coorg. That's Neil Gaiman and me for you.'

For two hours, there was no response from Neha, not even an emoji of acknowledgement. This was classic Neha. She was a disciplined food blogger who wrote every week without fail but was a little unreliable when it came to responding to a simple message. She was systematic and organized in most other aspects of her life—Rahul would readily admit to this—but terribly erratic when it came to personal correspondence.

Rahul and Neha had been in a relationship for two years. Theirs was a reasonably compatible relationship, but one that had also seen its mild ups and downs and on-off phases. For the last few weeks, however, Rahul had the uncomfortable feeling that the relationship had plateaued, and may actually be headed towards a downward gradient if nothing new happened. He wondered if his recent love of coffee could spark something new here as well.

Neha did reply eventually. It was a very short but clear message, 'OK! Let's go to Coorg, Rahul.'

Rahul responded instantly and expansively, 'I'm glad you are on board, Neha. I have a little brochure here that talks about Coorg and it looks really wonderful. The Kodava people, the Kaveri river, elephants and fruit bats, feasting, rice and pork, and lots of pure, fresh, coffee-laced air. And, of course, millions and millions of coffee beans. I have this fascination for coffee and I know you like it too. This holiday in Coorg will nurture our souls.'

'Not sure about the nurturing of our souls, Rahul. But I could do with a simple break—as far away from Mumbai as I can get. And Coorg is pretty good. Seems quiet and calm and peaceful. So, let's go.'

Many months later, Neha would wonder why she had used those words and would remind herself how unexpected life can be.

*

The unexpectedness began suddenly; in the small town of Gonikoppal, where Rahul and Neha stopped for a quick break and a hot cup of coffee. Until then, their journey towards Coorg had been uneventful and smooth. They had flown to Bengaluru airport and then hired a taxi. The car ride was relatively silent but then the driver abruptly launched into a monologue as they entered Mysore.

'Let me show you Mysore Palace. It's only a small detour, Sir, as this is a historic city of palaces. Here is the famous palace of the Wadiyar dynasty. Take a look. We don't need to get down from the car. This new palace was built where the old fort once stood, and after that there was the old palace which burnt down completely. I haven't seen it, Ma'am, but believe me it was there; I have seen some photographs. I am also proud to tell you that my great-grandfather was one of the builders of this new palace. Look at how grand it is. It looks incredibly beautiful when it is lit up at night during the Dussehra festival. And guess what my great-grandfather found when he was digging to build the foundations of this palace? He found an old gold coin buried in the sand. Maybe it was from the old fort from centuries ago. This coin has been with our family ever since. It is a great coin because it brings unexpected adventure always and sometimes fortune too, if you hold and observe it closely. I can tell you that it has brought my family quite a lot of adventure and a little fortune here and there, from time to time. So, let me show it to you. I have it right here in my purse.'

He took out a small coin with a hole in the centre and a visibly brass finish. 'Here is the gold coin. Look at it, Ma'am, Sir. Hold it. Do you see anything odd?'

21

Neha held the coin between her forefinger and thumb and then handed it over to Rahul. On one of the sides, Rahul spotted faded markings. He wasn't sure what they were. The other side of the coin had a distinct engraving of a bush. 'I think this is a coffee bush,' Rahul said. 'We are now very close to Coorg and maybe the kings of this place loved coffee too.'

The driver put the coin back into his wallet. The air was tangibly sweet as they drove away from Mysore and towards Coorg. On both sides of the road was lush green vegetation that stretched on endlessly. And there were forests too. Rahul slipped into a midday reverie imagining the beautiful advertisements he could create in this unspoilt land. Not too long after, they entered Gonikoppal.

It was at a roadside coffee shop here that they encountered the strange elderly lady. It seemed, as she approached, that she had a million wrinkles on her face. She wore a brown, nondescript saree. A little bent, but walking quite firmly, she held a packet wrapped in a local Kannada newspaper.

She came up to them, offered the packet to Rahul and said something long and involved. The driver was nice enough to translate. 'She wants to sell you this packet for a hundred rupees. She says it contains magical coffee beans from deep inside the forests. She also added that only she knows where these special beans of magic can be procured, and they are available only for a few weeks during the misty winter.'

The old woman piped up once again. They waited for her to finish and then the driver began to translate. 'She says that when you drink coffee brewed from these beans, magical things happen, experiences that money cannot buy. She knows this because she has seen such wondrous happenings. She is offering these beans to you for a highly discounted price because she likes both of you. She says that as soon as she saw you here, she knew that you were made for each other—both your bodies and minds. For each other and forever, she says.'

The last and somewhat intimate observation provoked Neha. 'How does she know when we don't know yet?' she asked Rahul. But before Rahul could respond, the old woman launched into another long story that the driver happily narrated.

'The last time she found these magical beans, deep inside the forest, was more than three years ago. She can spot them immediately, she says, because of their peculiar pink and purple shade. That is not the normal colour of ripe coffee beans, you know? The ripe beans are generally deep red and sometimes a nice shade of yellow but never pink and purple. She says she gifted these special beans to a plantation owner called Kariappa, who lives very close to this town. He was huge, a very large man who, the locals said, ate a lot of pork and drank copious amounts of brandy every day. But he was also an unhappy man because the coffee bushes on his plantation were constantly under attack from all sorts of pests, including a nasty borer. It didn't help that his married life wasn't in its best phase either, given his wife's depression.

'Kariappa paid this old woman two hundred rupees for these magical coffee beans. That's what she claims, but I think it is very unlikely. I can tell you that people in these parts are very careful about their money. I doubt she got more than fifty rupees.

23

Anyway, she says he made coffee from these special beans. He roasted and ground them, brewed the coffee and drank a big mugful one morning, hoping it would get rid of a particularly bad hangover. He also gave a cup to his wife and threw away the used coffee grounds on his plantations. Do you know what happened next?'

The driver paused here for effect. He looked at the old lady, then at Rahul and Neha, and resumed, 'What happened was totally unexpected, totally. His wife, that very evening, began dancing in the courtyard, full of joy and happiness, singing an old Hindi film song. Imagine this! Word got around quickly that Big Sir's madam had recovered from her sadness. The old woman here says that Kariappa's wife continues to be a very happy lady till this day. Apparently, at the last New Year's dance at Planters' Club, she danced the night away.'

Neha was now engrossed in the story and bubbling with questions, 'Did anything happen to the coffee bushes, the ones that weren't flourishing, on Kariappa's estate? I am sure something must have happened there.'

'Yes', said the driver, 'something magical happened there too. The old lady is about to narrate this part of the story.'

And so the story continued. 'As you know, Kariappa had thrown out the used coffee grounds on his plantation, after making the coffee that his wife and he had consumed. That night, he saw two foxes at the very spot where the grounds had been discarded. He saw them licking the grounds and then running wild around the plantation. The next morning, the borer disease that had infested his coffee bushes had vanished. Totally out of sight. The workers who were asked to keep an eye out came up to Kariappa and told him that they were amazed at the miracle that had happened overnight.

'Some of these workers then prostrated themselves at Kariappa's feet. They declared him a god for having brought about this miracle, one that had never been seen before on the coffee plantations in that area. They prayed that he bring miracles to their families too. There were a variety of prayers that the workers put forward. This old woman heard them because she was there too. Someone prayed for a grandfather to be cured of his bad gout, which was troubling him and leaving him grumpy all the time. Another prayed to bless a small five-year-old girl with the power of speech because she had not yet learnt to talk. One even prayed to bless a struggling woman with the gift of fertility.

'Kariappa, having woken up with a bad hangover that day after a particularly heavy night of spicy pork curry and bad brandy, was amazed but unfazed by these sudden prayers. His head was throbbing but he stared into the distance, and he listened. He offered his blessings quite generously to all the workers who had gathered there, waving his hands in benediction, and without holding back in any manner. Despite not being in any state to advise anyone, Kariappa meticulously blessed each person who put forth his or her prayers.

'He then asked them whether they had seen any foxes running around, and when they said they had not, he asked them to go away quietly, leave him alone and wait for their prayers to be fulfilled. The old woman says most of those prayers did come true, but not all. She says only the believers, those who believed fervently, saw their wishes come true. An orange tree grew at the spot where the coffee grounds had been discarded. She can show us this tree later in the day. But now, she asks again, do you wish to buy her coffee beans?'

Rahul Kamath, the writer of advertising stories and creator of the now-famous Nidra Hair Oil film, was amazed with this story about Kariappa, the magic coffee beans and the sad wife who turned happy forever. He wasn't sure if it was fact or fiction, but what an amazing treasure trove of stories anyway that he could put to use in the future. Amazing, really. This old lady was a superb storyteller, and their driver, bless him, a wonderful translator. Rahul, however, suspected that the driver had spiced up the story in translation, adding his own bits and pieces here and there.

'Let's buy these coffee beans,' Rahul said to the driver. 'Here's two hundred rupees for the old lady. Give her the money; tell her we are very grateful.'

'Don't do that, Sir,' the driver advised him. 'She will spend it on alcohol immediately.'

'Just go ahead,' Rahul said. 'Give her the money and give me this packet of beans. Let us leave this place before it gets dark and those foxes come around.'

The old lady counted the money and blessed them, not once but repeatedly, inspired perhaps by the great Kariappa's generous blessings. 'You will achieve, with these beans,' she said, 'what you have set out to achieve, although you may not know it yet.'

Rahul and Neha drove away from Gonikoppal on that peaceful afternoon carrying with them an exciting but dangerous packet that promised adventure and magic.

5

In a couple of hours, they arrived at Cottabetta Bungalow, located on top of a hill tucked deep within the coffee plantations of Pollibetta. There was a sudden chill in the air as they drove up the final stretch and the sprawling old bungalow came into view, chimney first. Then, a couple of hens crossed the road. Finally, the grey brick structure, with its vast verandah was visible. Serene, calm, picture-perfect.

Rahul had booked their stay at Cottabetta because he had loved the story of the place. This was once home to the director of the largest coffee plantation company in the area. He could almost see the big and powerful British coffee planters, and later the Indian directors, with stern expressions, big moustaches and khaki trousers, sipping strong coffee in the morning and even stronger whiskey in the evening. The first coffees of the season would have come to this bungalow, to be roasted here, examined with care and consumed with satisfaction, before they were eventually traded with the rest of the world, with the roasters of Italy and the cafés of Istanbul.

These thoughts had occupied Rahul's mind for the past couple of hours as they drove past acres and acres of coffee bushes and tall teak trees with green pepper vines snaking their way up. Would they see pictures of these great coffee planters and directors, perhaps even hear stories of their hardy lives and colourful adventures? Would they meet some old-timers with a taste for both coffee and gossip, who could be their guides to the rich history of this coffee paradise? What wonderful new coffees would he drink and enjoy here?

Neha, on the other hand, had nodded her way through most of the drive, lulled to sleep, no doubt, by the sweet coffee they had consumed at Gonikoppal. The bag of coffee beans that they had bought from the old woman lay by her side. Rahul was tempted, more than once, to bite into one of the beans, but he held himself back. *Let's roast the beans first when we get to Cottabetta*, he told himself.

They were greeted by two turbaned staff members when they reached the verandah of Cottabetta Bungalow. One of them was an old man with a long, wrinkled face and an expansive moustache. The other was a thin, strapping lad. Both of them were dressed in the same white and red uniform. The old man spoke in halting English.

'Sir and Madam, welcome to Cottabetta. A very warm and special welcome! I am Pooviah at your service. Look behind you and you will see the wonderful coffee hills.'

Rahul and Neha turned around. From their perch on top of Cottabetta Hill they could see coffee plantations everywhere, stretching on endlessly in all directions. The majestic mountains opened up around them and an unending carpet of heavenly green extended till wherever the eye could see. A little bird suddenly flew by. Neha, a keen birdwatcher, whispered excitedly, 'That's a red-whiskered bulbul, Rahul. The first one I've seen in ages. Wow! How beautiful is that.' Rahul looked at the bird as it flew away and wondered how Neha could have seen the red whiskers so quickly, that too in the fading light. *Women often see things that men never will*, he thought.

The old man, Pooviah, spoke again. 'From your room you can see the Cottabetta coffee estate. It is a most wonderful view, Sir. But please do shut your door firmly at night because sometimes we have visitors. Elephants and one ghost too, Sir.'

'Elephants and *one* ghost!' Rahul and Neha were understandably alarmed.

'Yes, Sir. But gentle elephants and a very kind ghost. They may wake you up and disturb your sleep, but they have never harmed anyone,' Pooviah explained kindly.

'I can understand elephants, Pooviah, they were mentioned on the website too. But a ghost? I didn't see details of ghosts on your brochure. Tell me, is this a haunted house, or is this part of some scare-and-adventure routine?'

'No, no, Sir. This ghost does not haunt us at all. Never. He doesn't even appear in front of everyone. He only speaks to people who love coffee as much as he did, never to anyone else. We call him the coffee ghost. He was a very old English coffee planter, Sir, who loved these plantations with all his heart. Scott Ramsey was his name, Sir. My father knew him. I can show you his grave tomorrow, if you wish.'

Rahul and Neha looked at each other apprehensively. *Should they stay?* Ghosts were obviously not real, except ghosts of one's own past, which kept appearing from time to time. And Pooviah was very old, old enough to imagine and believe such things.

'Have you ever actually seen this ghost?' Rahul asked Pooviah and the younger man.

The young man spoke up. 'No, Sir. None of us have seen him. But some others have told us that they have.' This reassured Rahul. He took Neha's hand and walked to their room in the cottage.

It was a splendid room, dominated by a magnificent four-poster bed and a broad rosewood couch. Before they turned in for the night, Rahul handed over the old woman's bag of pink coffee beans to Pooviah and asked him to roast them. 'A dark roast would be nice. I would like to drink some of this coffee tomorrow morning,' he said. Pooviah nodded, opened the bag and smelt the beans, and then quickly wrapped up the bag once again. Rahul somehow missed the startled expression on the man's wrinkled face.

*

Somewhere in the middle of the night, in one corner of Rahul and Neha's bedroom, sat the coffee ghost. He sat on a chair, very silently, totally unseen. He had a big white head that was well formed, almost perfectly round, with a mop of grey hair. His eyes, nostrils and ears were totally and clearly visible. He wore spectacles—an old-fashioned broad, thick plastic pair that was perched squat on the bridge of his big nose. He wore a pocket watch too, the dangling silver chain of which was secured to the loop of his belt.

But the most important feature of the apparition was the large, white mug that he clutched in his right hand. A mug of steaming hot black coffee. Every few minutes, he raised the mug to his mouth and sipped with quiet satisfaction. If you went close, you could actually smell the delicious, strong aromas of medium-roasted robusta coffee from Coorg. If you went even closer, you could detect mild notes of orange and pepper, fruits native to the region.

Looking closely at the coffee ghost (only if he made himself visible to you because ghosts have the power to choose who can see them, and they are totally invisible to the rest of the world), you could even detect a thin smile on his face as he drank his coffee. He could tell that Rahul was a great lover of coffee. Years of haunting experience had honed his instinct in that regard. If he were being totally honest, he would have to admit that the transfer of the bag of coffee beans between Rahul and Pooviah, which he had witnessed, had also fed his instinct on this particular occasion.

The coffee ghost was thinking that here, finally, was a companion worth speaking to, getting to know and sharing coffee talk with. Ghosts are terribly lonely and so, when they think they have good company, it means the world to them. The ghost smiled and watched them sleep.

Rahul rolled over in his bed. He inched closer to Neha, threw a relaxed arm over her and retreated into deep slumber again. The coffee ghost sighed, thinking of the only woman in his own life—Alyssa, lady of charm, lady of enchantment, lady of love. She was long gone but remained forever in his mind. He took another sip of coffee, looked deep into his mug and then vanished into the night.

6

The next morning, before the sun rose over the hills nearby, Rahul and Neha slipped into their shorts and sneakers, and strolled into the coffee plantation just outside the Cottabetta Bungalow. It was cold and the leaves of the coffee bushes stood very still. The plantations ahead of them ran on endlessly, but because of the heavy canopies and tall shrubs that surrounded them, it felt as if they were deep within the heart of a forest. Neha brushed her fingers against the sparkling drops of dew that sat on some of these green leaves. The drops instantly collapsed and Neha proceeded to lick the dew. She liked doing that.

'Try it, Rahul. This is a refreshing taste with a hint of delicate sweetness. It reminds me of very light tender coconut water. And it's also sharp on your tongue, maybe because it is so raw and fresh. I wonder if we collect thousands of these drops carefully, can we package them into a natural drink of sorts, straight from the leaves and trees? We can call them Coffee Dew Drops, or something like that. Bound to be a market for that kind of a drink. What do you think?'

Neha was a food blogger and Rahul knew from her tone that she had her thinking cap on. Sometimes, she could write as many as seven blogs in a single day. And if you were with her during such fluent periods, it was prudent to stay silent and let her quill flow. So, he just listened as she continued happily.

'You know what? We could pair this dew drop drink with coffee. One could sip a little bit of coffee, then wash it down with Coffee Dew Drops. Then your next sip of coffee, and so on. Hey, Rahul, here's a great new thought bubbling in my head. Why always pair a drink with food? Why not pair a drink with another drink? I mean, we could have cappuccino and dew drops, or even a smoky single malt paired with clear, sweet dew drops. What a nice idea! I am going to write about this fantasy in my next blog.'

Rahul looked at her. *It was indeed a new idea, though an unclear one*, he thought. He didn't see the purpose of pairing one drink with another. Food was paired with drink so that you could wash it down. How could two drinks do that kind of thing to each other? But he listened intently because Neha was talking with a lot of enthusiasm. Until, at that very moment, he saw the ghost.

The ghost came out from behind a tree very quietly. He had a translucent body, a big white head with a mop of salt-and-pepper hair and thick spectacles. He held a large white mug in his hand with steam rising from it. He smiled at Rahul and raised his mug as a friendly gesture. Rahul's jaw and eyes dropped. He stared and stood transfixed. His heart skipped a few beats, which is not unusual for people who unexpectedly run into ghosts. His first instinct was to run.

'Hey, Neha! Let's run! There's a ghost out here.'

Startled, Neha stopped her commentary. She looked around; she could see no ghost, but she ran, holding Rahul's hand. Both of them dashed at a fast and desperate clip. Running and running, the two of them, for a moment, forgot the ghost and zigzagged between bushes and mud pathways. Rahul realized that it had been a while since the two of them had been holding hands so tight, and for so long. After they reached a clearing, Rahul paused and smiled, looking at Neha. But he had been so engrossed in holding her hand while running that they had slowed down and the ghost had caught up with them. So, they ran again, faster this time.

The coffee ghost followed, floating casually behind them. He then spoke in the voice of Scott Ramsey, planter and lover of coffee, long dead but now alive. It was a deep voice, layered with reassurance.

'Rahul, don't be afraid of me. It seems you love coffee very much. I know of your daily visits to the Starbucks café at Horniman Circle, Rahul. I want to speak to you about coffee. That's all I want to do, really. Coffee has been my entire life, you know? Sit down for a moment beneath any of these shady trees. Let me speak to you. I am a ghost all right, that is for sure, but I will do you no harm. None at all.'

It was an endearing tone, one that made Rahul consider halting for a moment, but his legs wouldn't stop running and his hands wouldn't stop pulling Neha along. He was still fearful because he had never encountered a ghost before. And there was Neha, panting yet keeping up with him. *Should I consider speaking to this strange apparition? More importantly, how does he know about me and Starbucks?*

Perhaps sensing that Rahul would not stop, the coffee ghost continued to follow them, now taking on a storytelling voice. What neither Rahul nor Neha had realized was that the ghost, if it wanted to, could have caught up with them long back, because floating is faster than running. But he had chosen to maintain the distance.

'Let me tell you a nice story about coffee, Rahul. Don't miss out on this. Listen to me because God knows that of all people, you will really like it,' and then with a calculated thought, the ghost added, 'It may even give you an idea for your next film.'

What is happening? How does he know about my film project? How long has he been stalking me?

'In these parts of Coorg lives an old woman called Bhagya. Hers is a beautiful name because not only is it easy on the ears but it also means good fortune. Bhagya is very, very old. She was here when I was alive, sixty years ago. Some people I know claim that she is more than 400 years of age, that she is the oldest living person in the world, but I ask, how is that possible? I don't know. I see her every now and then, near Gonikoppal, near Pollibetta, and near many other towns in these parts. The locals here will tell you that she is very, very sharp. And guess what! She is always on the lookout for coffee beans with special magic in them.'

Rahul slowed down a little. His ears perked up. He remembered the old woman from Gonikoppal who had sold him the pink coffee beans for Rs 200. He recalled the story of planter Kariappa's sad wife who had been instantly transported into a state of great happiness by these beans.

The coffee ghost continued. 'Once, Bhagya gifted a bag of coffee beans to a young couple who worked on these plantations and had an infant at home. This couple was known to love coffee and roasted their own beans at home. She asked them to brew coffee from these beans and serve it to the infant for a minimum of one week. She told them that the beans were from an estate whose owner was a great man of science and spirituality from Japan, and a lover of education too. The coffee would bring the child good fortune and great success; this was a gift because she loved the child very much. They were hesitant but eventually persuaded to accept the beans after Bhagya assured them that the beans would ensure the child's life was very successful. Do you know what happened then?'

Rahul, the film-maker who always loved a good story, was unable to contain himself. He broke his silence and exclaimed, 'No, I don't know. Tell me, I am listening.'

'Are you speaking to me, Rahul?' asked Neha, still clutching his hand. 'What do you want me to tell you? Is that bloody ghost gone, or was it a touch of sunshine that got into your head, as usual?' That is when Rahul realized that Neha couldn't see the ghost.

'Listen to his story, Neha,' said Rahul. And then, turning to the ghost, he said, 'Speak louder, whoever you are. Let my friend Neha hear you too!'

Upon hearing this, the coffee ghost spoke louder and in a very different tone and frequency. Now, Neha could hear him too.

'The infant loved the coffee. They fed him tiny spoonfuls for ten days. Each time the coffee touched the baby's tongue, he would gurgle and smile and slurp. Each time, he would shake his tiny fists with joy, clenching them tightly together and opening his eyes wide. Surely, something was up. And then the coffee beans were over and everyone forgot about the old woman. The child was named Rama Bhadra. At the age of five, Rama solved difficult mathematics problems. A week after his tenth birthday, he was selected for the National Science Scholarship. At fifteen, they measured his IQ and it was well over Mensa levels, a few notches above Einstein too, I am told. At the age of seventeen, RB (as he was called then) received admission offers from five Ivy League universities in America. He chose Princeton. Now, he is a distinguished professor of theoretical physics there. In fact, he is tipped to win the Nobel Prize soon. Imagine! The child of uneducated, simple coffee plantation workers is now amongst the most brilliant physicists in the world. Those coffee beans did something to his brain; they brought him good fortune, just as old Bhagya had predicted. Oh yes, there was magic in them.'

The coffee ghost paused here for effect. Ghosts, over their long years, hone their expertise in narrating haunting stories. And then he said, 'Rahul and Neha, I can tell you many more lovely coffee stories, about Bhagya and many others. Coffee beans have all the magic in the world, you know. I am a harmless ghost. I am lonely. I want to speak to you. You can call me RG. RG for Ramsey's Ghost. Speak to me, walk with me and I will add a lot to your extreme love of coffee.'

*

So began an intense friendship between Rahul, Neha and RG.

'I know you met old Bhagya on the way here,' RG said to Rahul and Neha later that day. 'And I know she sold you a bag of special coffee beans. She does that only for people whom she likes. I saw this bag of beans last night on Pooviah's kitchen table. I looked inside and recognized the coffee beans immediately. Do you know where they are from?'

'Perhaps from that drunken planter Kariappa's estate,' said Rahul. 'Maybe Bhagya stole them when Kariappa was sloshed. She looked like an old, wrinkled, experienced thief, if you ask me. An expert thief of coffee beans.'

'No, Rahul. Bhagya is not a petty thief. She is a giver of fortune. These pink and purple coffee beans she has bestowed upon you come from a small plantation called Edobetta which was originally set up by a Buddhist monk from Japan. Actually, it was the only Japanese-owned plantation in Coorg—not any more though because the monk is dead and gone. He named it Edobetta because 'Edo' is the ancient and sacred Japanese name for Tokyo, his city. Strange name, if you ask me. I remember meeting him when I was alive and kickin' and he was a good man, oh yes, and a good friend too. Shaved head, orange robes, perpetually chanting, the full monk monty. He loved his drink too, strong and neat. Actually, to tell you the truth, I am not sure if he was a genuine monk either, though he took care to look like one in every way. I never really knew why he settled down here when Japan is such a beautiful place. But he grew a special kind of pink coffee beans using plant material that he had carried all the way from Tokyo. It is so very different from our own robustas and arabicas. I remember his name quite clearly: Saito.'

Saito. The name rings a bell, Rahul thought. And then he knew why. The name reminded him of Yamamato, the Japanese inventor whose patented springs were generously used by Nippon Springlove for their mattresses; the same company which now wanted a great advertisement from him to popularize its revolutionary beds amongst the Indian masses who seek firm new mattresses for their sore backs; the very same company whose owner had most generously offered to share as much as 10 per cent of his revenues with the advertising agency. He recalled Haroon's words: 'This deal will make us very rich, Rahul.'

RG continued speaking. 'So, when you drink this coffee today, Rahul and Neha, sit back on the cane chair on the porch of the bungalow and enjoy what follows. Surprising and positive things will happen. When you love such great coffee, great things can happen.'

7

As the day progressed into evening, Pooviah brought them their coffee in a pot with two cups on the side. RG had vanished a couple of hours ago, presumably back to his haunt for a touch of ghostly rest. Rahul no longer feared the ghost though Neha still refrained from speaking to it. Pooviah laid the pot down on a cane table and spoke.

'Sir, I made this coffee from that bag of beans you gave. It's not like I opened them earlier, Sir, but the smell . . . it is rather odd yet beautiful. Not like our coffees; not at all. Enjoy, Sir and Madam. But just be careful.' Pooviah stared at them for a moment and then left.

The coffee was softly sweet and refreshing. And then, slowly, they sensed the nutty aroma——of walnuts, mild but deliciously bitter. Rahul knew from his readings about coffee that such a delicate sweetness could only come from a fully ripened coffee berry that had been carefully picked and pulped on the ground under bright, clean summer sunshine. Because then the richness of the raw soil would mingle with the golden heat of the sand and soak in the sun to create this rare, luxurious and nutty taste.

The myriad tastes of coffee continued to amaze him, each one so different from the previous and each teasing the senses so delicately. He decided to use this opportunity to educate Neha, who sat nice and close by his side.

'How do you like the old lady's coffee, Neha? Isn't it so beautiful? Can you taste the walnuts?'

There was no response. So, he asked her again. He turned to find Neha sprawled across the cane sofa in deep slumber. *She was awake a few minutes ago. When had she fallen asleep, that too so deeply?* He shook her, but she was like a log, muscles locked and eyes shut.

Then, without any warning, he felt sleep overcome him too. From far away, it penetrated his body through his eyes, swimming in like a gentle cloud. It narrowed his eyes when it came in and brought a general sense of growing calm that wasn't there seconds ago. There was a tender but overpowering silence that it cast on him, which was impossible to counter with words, hands or legs, because they were going dead too. In this twilight zone before deep sleep, the mind has no thoughts because it goes pleasantly numb in anticipation of the rest ahead. *We love sleep, don't we?*

Rahul could feel himself levitating. He saw the coffee cup on the cane table going farther and farther away, initially a sharp image, but hazy after a few seconds. It then looked like the cup was being taken away by Pooviah or by someone else with a red and white turban; it did not really matter because within a few seconds he too was deep in sleep.

He woke up almost immediately, not in Cottabetta Bungalow or his familiar room in Mumbai, but in some place that looked like a very small café. There were people around him who looked like they were Japanese, seated on low wooden tables, speaking in Japanese and drinking coffee. The entire place smelt of coffee. Neha was there too, sitting by his side, her left hand resting softly on his lap. On the wall was a beautiful painting of a monkey on a horse, with Mount Fuji in the background. A lady in a red and golden kimono came around with white coffee mugs on a lovely looking oval wooden tray.

As the bright red of her dress approached them, she spoke in highly accented English. 'Welcome back, Rahul-san and Neha-san. Will you have your usual coffee today?' She then bowed before them. *Are we in Japan?* Rahul thought.

How did this Japanese woman know their names? Where were they, really? *Always best to clarify matters before doing anything*, thought Rahul. 'Thank you, gracious lady,' he said, bringing up his best manners and bowing in reciprocation. 'Can you please tell me where we are now?'

'This is your favourite café, Rahul-san, the Mayaso Coffee Shop,' the woman replied, taken by surprise. Then, she chose to add, 'Your guests just called me. They will be arriving shortly and have been apologizing profusely for the delay.'

Rahul quickly decided that he must play the part, which appeared to be the only productive path forward. 'Yes, of course, gracious lady,' he responded, 'we will wait patiently for our guests. And we will have our usual coffee now. We love the coffee here; it is so different from what we get at home.'

She served them their coffee in the white mugs. When they sipped a little bit, they felt the same nutty aroma and mild walnutty taste coming back immediately. That plantation monk must actually have been from Tokyo, and if this was RG's story coming true, then great things would happen soon. This time around there was also an underlying almond-like flavour, which Rahul immediately recognized as a hallmark of very carefully roasted coffee.

*

Their guests arrived within a few minutes. They were two Japanese gentlemen, both completely bald and wearing rimmed spectacles. They bowed, apologized profusely for being late and then bowed again. 'Rahul-san, we were held up because of a bad motor accident near Black Gate. We are so sorry, really. But now we are here and ready to talk to you. I am Takahira Yamamoto and this is my brother, Shinko Yamamoto. We are here just for you.'

Yamamoto again! Rahul looked at them startled. *This name again?* It was a splendid title—pedigreed Japanese name for sure, he had no doubt about that. But how was it that the inventor of the mattress springs and these two bald men had the same name? And then there was the coffee monk who also had a Japanese name, Saito. So many Japanese were suddenly entering his life. It was truly odd. Was this the effect of those magical coffee beans, or did it have something to do with RG?

At this point, Takahira Yamamoto spoke again. 'We will talk to you, Rahul-san, and give you all the information you need, but not here. It cannot be done here. This is a very crowded café and people are always eavesdropping. We will take you to a nice, private place just down this road. We will take you to Yanaka-reien. There we can speak amongst all the happy spirits and silent graves.'

Rahul and Neha quickly exchanged glances, now with increasing concern. Happy spirits? Silent graves? Where were these Japanese strangers preparing to lead them?

As if on cue, the other Yamamoto, Shinko, spoke. 'Yanaka-reien is our sacred cemetery, my friends. Good things invariably happen there. You will find graves and black cats—and tons of good luck. We will be alone amongst many dead people. There we can speak our minds freely.' Then, suddenly, he changed the tone of his voice. 'We must go now. People are watching us closely. Anything can happen here.'

Alarmed, Rahul and Neha stood up immediately and followed the brothers to Yanaka-reien. They walked in complete silence. As they approached their destination, they first spotted many green trees and then a small sign that marked out the graveyard. Rahul and Neha were taken aback to see how well-maintained the place was. No weeds here, but lots of well-tended trees and bushes, fresh greenery all around and broad winding roads going deep into the heart of the huge graveyard. It was almost like a beautiful park with much foliage. And then, right in front of them were hundreds of tombstones, all looking well-rested.

Shinko Yamamoto spoke again, but in a very low voice that was respectful of their surroundings. 'Rahul-san, this is Yanaka-reien, which translates to Yanaka Spirit Park. We have brought you here with a purpose. This is the final resting place of more than seven thousand great spirits. This park covers over twenty-five acres. If you get lost here, it is difficult to find out exactly where you are, so please do not leave us and wander away. Now, look around carefully before we begin speaking and tell me what you see.'

They looked around. Some of the graves appeared to be ancient by the look of the stones and the blackish moss on them. Some others looked modern with very vibrant designs adorning them, which are generally not associated with the dead. Most of the graves were topped with beautiful flowers, arranged in very pleasing patterns. A number of cherry trees lined the road ahead, their branches waving slowly in a warm welcome. A mild afternoon sun peeped through these branches, casting its soft shadows on some of the tombstones. Just ahead of them, a black cat with sharp green eyes crossed the road and went on to sit near a grave in a grassy spot that it seemed to know very well. As it sat close to the gravestone, its body appeared to relax immediately. *Reaching home does that to us all*, thought Rahul.

He spoke to the Yamamotos, holding Neha's hand the entire time. 'I see a beautiful graveyard. Extremely well maintained. This must be the best kept graveyard in the world. Actually, it is more like a wonderful garden that we can roam around in to calm our nerves.' Neha, whose anxiety was shooting through the roof amidst all the perplexing and sudden drama, wondered at the irony.

'What else?' asked one of the Yamamotos.

'I see total peace and quiet. The sort of peace that comes with deep, well-rested sleep.'

Both the gentlemen nodded vigorously and replied together, quickly, virtually in one voice, with a heavy Japanese accent, 'That's absolutely correct, Rahul-san. That's exactly why we brought you here. Now, listen carefully. In this graveyard lies Yoshinobu Tokugawa, the last shogun of Japan. He was a great and imposing man. Let us take you to his grave.'

They walked a little and stopped near a grand section of Yanaka-reien, fenced off from the rest of the cemetery. The grave inside was beautifully crafted with smooth granite and topped with small, white stones. They looked in through imposing metal gates that were shut.

After a few minutes of silence, during which they admired the grand grave, Shinko resumed speaking, 'Yoshinobu was born in 1837. He was the fifteenth and last shogun of the Tokugawa shogunate. He was the sole Tokugawa shogun who did not step into our capital city of Edo. Something like that would have been unthinkable before him. He carried out many urgent reforms, including a massive cleaning up of the government. He also won fierce battles as commander of the Imperial Palace's defence. But in 1867, he resigned as shogun and handed power back to the then emperor. What happened after that is more interesting, which is actually the subject of our story here and why we have brought you to his grave.

'After his reign as shogun, Yoshinobu led a quiet, calm and happy retired life. He pursued many interesting hobbies—archery, hunting, cycling, photography. Yes, his photography skills were quite renowned and many of his photographs have been published too. But of all these interests, Yoshinobu pursued

47

with most passion his love of coffee. The last shogun of our land had an extreme love for coffee.'

Rahul's ears immediately perked up at this, and he listened intently.

'What is not commonly known, Rahul-san, is that Yoshinobu was actually the first Japanese to taste and savour coffee. So you could say that he was the man who brought the taste of coffee to Japan, the original inspiration for Mayaso Coffee Shop, which we have just left, and thousands of other cafés that we love today. He indulged in coffee on a daily basis and voiced his opinions on the drink quite vociferously. When he was shogun, he obtained the best and most flavourful coffees from across the world and served them to his guests. In 1867, when he hosted delegates from Europe at Osaka Castle with a magnificent banquet, he brought the meal to an end with a most delicious cup of the beverage. This special coffee was talked about for many months and days. The coffee beans he had used were unique and secret. Some even say they were magical.

'Then, well before he died, what Yoshinobu did will surprise you. To preserve this special coffee for future generations, he shared the secret of these special beans with just one person, a Japanese monk called Saito, whom he knew very well, a sort of personal drinking partner if you will. A few years later, Saito vanished from Japan. We have read that he went away to India, to your great country, and planted this special coffee there in a beautiful area near the western mountains where coffee grows abundantly. He was never seen in our country again.'

Rahul and Neha looked at each other. This was totally surreal—RG's story about the Japanese monk and his magical coffee, the old woman and her magical pink coffee beans, and now this. Rahul was starting to get really worried now; nothing seemed to make sense except that it was obvious that all of it was connected in some strange way. What magic had brought them here, to this distant graveyard in Tokyo, to the grave of a shogun they had never heard about before?

Shinko Yamamoto continued. 'Yoshinobu lived life to the fullest, well into his grand old years. He was a very fit man who, until his very last days, went about hunting, shooting and cycling with a lot of energy, discipline and passion. Legend has it that the main reason behind his fitness was the mattress he slept on, a very firm bed that kept him so sprightly. This special bed kept his back absolutely intact, very flexible and in mint condition, even with all that arduous physical activity, which sadly cannot be said for many people these days. All this is spoken about, Rahul-san, but we will never know for sure. What we do know is that my father, the respected Yamamoto, was inspired by Yoshinobu and this legend of his fabulous, flexible back, to invent a special spring technology for firm beds that specially protect the back. He spent seven years perfecting this great invention, working all by himself. He said to us, to me and my brother here, that this spring is designed in such a beautiful manner, such a unique mechanical way, that anyone sleeping on these beds will keep their backs wonderfully flexible and relaxed forever. And he gifted the first bed made using this technology to Yoshinobu himself.

'We have also heard rumours that our father was secretly in touch with Yoshinobu's spirit after he died, and that the dead shogun actually served as his mentor and guide. During one of these séances with the dead, Yoshinobu also spoke to our father about a great treasure that he had once owned, which he wanted to leave to our father for all his services. He said he had locked away the treasure and entrusted this task to a monk, but that monk had run away with the keys. We gathered this must be none other than Saito. Our beloved father told us bits of this story from time to time, but he did not live to tell us the entire tale. He was so focused on further developing his new spring technology that it consumed his entire life. He worked at his laboratory day and night, until, one day, he suddenly collapsed and died. What wonderful technology he created and constantly improved and perfected, which is now used so widely for the firmest and best beds across the world!'

Rahul's jaw dropped as he tried to comprehend all this. His mind was spinning.

Shinko spoke again, bringing his story to an end, 'We were guided to meet you here today, Rahul-san, and to share this story with you. Now, let us all pay our respects to Yoshinobu Tokugawa at this peaceful grave of our last shogun.'

They bowed and stayed like that for some time. A greyish-white cat appeared from nowhere and looked at them intently. 'That means good luck,' said Takahira Yamamoto. 'When a grey cat looks at us like that, it means that we will find the treasure that we seek in life. Yes, we will surely find it, Rahul-san. Here, take this small coin with you as a token of good luck and a cherished memory of this very famous grave.' It was a small round brass coin with a hole in the centre and Japanese markings. Rahul could not see it clearly. He pulled out his wallet and put the coin into it without a second thought. They then bowed to each other, the sort of deep bows that the Japanese simply love.

After that, the Yamamoto brothers did not say a single word but walked them out of Yanaka-reien, back to Mayaso Coffee Shop, on the same road, below the same cherry trees, in complete silence. Rahul and Neha walked slowly, reflecting on the strange story they had just heard.

On reaching the Mayaso Coffee Shop, the two bald Yamamotos left instantly. The same waitress came around and offered them the same black coffee in the same white mugs once again. It was the same nutty flavours that they could recognize well by now. They slowly sipped the coffee. For a minute, Rahul and Neha looked deep into each other's eyes and liked what they saw there—reflections of a future that looked nice and fuzzy and forever. Then they held hands softly and fell into a deep, very deep sleep.

8

When they woke up, they were back on the cane sofas in the verandah at Cottabetta Bungalow. There was no trace of Mayaso Coffee Shop or anything remotely Japanese. The sun was setting over the coffee plantations, splashing orange hues over the green canopy in front of them. Their empty cups of coffee were right in front and their minds felt calm and relaxed. Neha turned to Rahul.

'Rahul, I dreamt we were in a graveyard in Tokyo. Do you think it could be a hallucination? Or did we really visit Japan? Oh my God, whatever it was, I am so glad that you were with me.'

'I dreamt exactly the same thing, Neha, and I am so happy you were with me too. That old lady's coffee is having an effect on us. I think RG is right. Those beans have magic in them.'

'Rahul, did we meet two bald Japanese guys called Yama-something? Is that true as well?'

'Absolutely yes, Neha! The Yamamoto brothers, the bald and bespectacled sons of Yamamoto, the inventor of the famous and unique bed spring. We did meet them and they took us to the shogun's grave. I think this meeting was arranged by someone—

but I don't know who—for a very good reason. This was good magic with a purpose. Now I think I have with me the storyline for a brilliant advertisement for Nippon Springlove. I was searching for it and now it's come into my head. Haroon will love this. Oh yes, I know he will love it.'

That very evening, after a nice, quiet dinner of Coorgi pork curry and rice (it was spicy and had to be tempered with some yoghurt at the end), Rahul sat at the old writing desk in the bungalow, opened his laptop and began writing his story for the Nippon Springlove film. He typed furiously like a man possessed.

EXTRA-DARK BATTLEFIELD: NIGHT SCENE

HARUTO, Japanese male (mid-thirties to early forties) tall, fit, muscular, neatly trimmed royal beard and clad in royal armour, has his katana drawn out. He is on a horse and has a banner attached to it. There is total darkness, with a tinge of red behind him.

Haruto does not blink, his eyes are fixated on his goal—right in front of him. He has an excellent posture and a serious demeanour. As he raises his sword, a horde of soldiers, garbed in armour inferior to his, ride out on their horses—all in majestic slow motion.

In a series of quick cuts we see the following:

- *Haruto wields his katana at the enemy from atop his horse.*
- *Haruto, now on foot, elbows an enemy soldier who rushes towards him.*
- *Haruto stands tall above the opposing warrior, who falls to his knees, witnessing his defeat right in front of him.*

•   *Haruto plants his banner into the soil and looks gallant and determined in front of his army.*

                                  CUT TO:

                    INT. CASTLE CHAMBERS—NIGHT

Royal paintings adorn the stone walls of the gigantic room. A goze (minstrel), sitting comfortably in a corner of the room, sings and plays a beautiful song on a koto.

    Three concubines, young and voluptuous, walk into the room, in front of a weary yet happy Haruto. They are dressed in beautiful silk kimonos—pink, red and blue. He smiles at KUNIKO—dressed in pink—and she smiles back coyly.

                    INT. HARUTO'S ROOM—NIGHT

A large, handmade painting of Mt Fuji and a four-poster bed greet Haruto as he walks into his royal room. He smiles after entering.

                                  CUT TO:

Three complete sets of armour, the same as what Haruto had donned in the battlefield, stand tall as our protagonist sits on his comfortable mattress and pats it twice. He takes off and looks at his headpiece, the last bit of armour he had on, with satisfaction. He lies down for a moment on the mattress, just to feel its fabulous comfort and fit.

    The camera pans to reveal the back of his body, now in a sleeping posture on the mattress. His spine has adjusted very well, the mattress has adjusted perfectly to the contours of Haruto's body. As Haruto sits

up, *cools down and relaxes—his narration starts here—in Japanese,
with English subtitles at the bottom.*

HARUTO (V.O.)

*I fight many wars, and I win them all. I shoot, I hunt, I lead a very
active life. I exercise choices in so many things. For all this, I have
to protect my back and body, and make sure they are in great shape.
So, for the mattress I sleep on, there is only one choice and no other.
Nippon Springlove, developed by my friend and scientist, Yamamoto.
The special spring in this mattress keeps my back in perfect shape,
relaxed and fit every single day and night.*

*Haruto now sips tea from a royal, but minimalist, cup and notices
Kuniko as she enters the room—slowly and seductively, with a hand
fan covering a portion of her smiling face. Haruto smiles back at her
as she approaches him.*

DISSOLVE TO:

*Cut to a panoramic view of the mattress now; graphical introduction
of a giant, golden metal spring—it slowly emerges from the mattress
as the background turns dark and the lights go off.*

DEEP-VOICED NARRATOR (V.O.)

*Nippon Springlove. Specially developed and patented by the great
Yamamoto in Japan, for the shogun himself. A great scientific leap in*

mattresses, with a patented spring that totally protects your back and gives you deep and restful sleep, worthy of the warrior in you.

CUT TO BLACK

The name NIPPON SPRINGLOVE and its logo appear on the screen. The logo is in a Japanese-like font. The brand's byline fades into the screen, right underneath the logo. It reads, 'Sleep like a Shogun'.

Rahul paused here. He was happy with the way the script had worked out. He loved the line 'Sleep like a shogun'. He knew right away that this was a winning line. It immediately signalled at the Japanese technology in this marvellous mattress. It also implied warrior-like fitness, for which deep sleep was essential. Also, the line had a very nice ring to it. Sleep like a shogun. Wow! Well done, Rahul. Then, as an afterthought, he added:

The film could possibly end by showing the shogun waking up the next morning, looking very relaxed, patting his mattress and sipping on coffee from a white steaming mug offered to him by the beautiful, graceful, kimono-clad Kuniko. This is an optional ending.

Before he slept that night, he emailed the script to Haroon. 'Hi, Haroon. Here's my script for Nippon Springlove. It's magical. Let me know what you think. Cheers. Rahul.'

The very next morning, even before he could wake up, Haroon's response was waiting in his inbox. 'Hi, Rahul. What a superb film, man. It works beautifully for me. I am taking it across to the Nippon Springlove guy at lunch today. I will tell you what he says. I suspect we'll soon be rich. Enjoy your holiday, shogun. Haroon.'

And then, later that afternoon, came another email from the boss. 'Hi, Rahul. Mr Nippon Springlove just loved the script. He is raving about it. We drank two beers together and he wanted a third. I think we have a winner. The guy wants to meet you when you are back. He wants to know where this powerful idea came from. He also asked me what concubines were, and we bonded well over this subject because you know that I know this particular topic well enough. By the way, he has reconfirmed that he will give our company a 10 per cent share of the revenues for the next five years in exchange for this advertisement. What a sweet deal, shogun. We will be rich; we will all be rich; I am telling you. By the way, he is also sending us two more Nippon Springlove king-sized mattresses today as tokens of appreciation. Where shall I keep yours, shogun? Haroon.'

And then again, in the evening, came one more email. 'Hi, Rahul. I am excited. This will make us rich and famous. I have already found a director to make this film, but he needs some time. So, you can extend your holiday if you want to. After writing about the shogun and his concubines, you may want to visit Japan. Who knows what you will find there? I can pay for the tickets. Cheers. Haroon.' He clearly was a satisfied and happy man.

Behind Rahul, a pair of eyes appeared, somewhat ghostly. It was RG who knew that this adventure had just begun, but he was getting a little worried about where Rahul was headed.

9

The next day, as they were ambling through the coffee bushes, Neha started speaking.

'You know, Rahul, that entire Japan thing was weird. Those coffee beans have something really powerful and wonderful in them. God knows what is packed into them. I mean, how else did we end up in Tokyo, of all places a graveyard there, and then back here? How is it that both of us went through the exact same story in our dreams, or maybe it was totally real? Can the two of us actually share a dream? Is that physically, or even metaphysically, possible? And that Japanese monk Saito, he is the root cause of all this because he picked up those unusual coffee beans from the shogun and brought them to India, and then the old lady stole some of them and sold them to us. That's what that other weird guy, that planter's ghost, told us. Oh! And those weird, bald Yamamotos. Where did they come from and where did they go? We are getting mixed up with too many weird people and things, Rahul. Not a good sign.'

'I see your point, Neha. It is weird, but it is happening, don't you see? Maybe both of us, deep down, really wanted a real adventure away from the humdrum of our routines, the sameness of our Mumbai lives. If that's the case, and maybe it is, then our desire is playing out now IMAX size. We've got ghosts, graveyards, old witches who steal and bald men who vanish. What more do you need for a great adventure? And by the way, just by the way, this quick Japan visit also helped me write a beautiful story for the mattress film last night, about which Haroon says the owner of Nippon Springlove is thrilled. Haroon also says we are very rich now because Mr Nippon will pay us handsomely for the film. And he says the owner has also sent me an additional Nippon mattress yesterday. It should come in handy, I think.'

Neha blushed a little and then spoke again. 'That is brilliant, Rahul. I mean, the film. When can I read the killer script?'

'Any time, Neha, any time. I wrote it last night, sent it out and immediately fell asleep. But hey, Neha, listen. I don't think this adventure is really about the mattresses. That too, but that's not it, really. Somewhere, it is the coffee that is driving us. Just think about it, Neha. It started when I was drinking an Americano at Starbucks. Then the coffee plantation bungalow here in Coorg. The old lady and her pink coffee beans. The story of the drunk coffee planter. Mayaso Coffee Shop, yes, I remember that name, near the graveyard in Tokyo. The shogun who first tasted coffee in Japan. The coffee monk Saito. And, to top it all, a coffee ghost. This is all about coffee, and it is leading us somewhere, Neha. I can feel it in my bones. Everything tends to have a purpose, even if it is so deep and submerged that we don't see it for some time.'

'Do you think we can ask RG, the coffee ghost? Maybe he knows something more.'

'Well, if RG appears any time soon, we will ask him for sure. He is the talkative sort anyway.'

RG was following them as keenly as a ghost could, so he appeared instantly.

'Hi, Rahul and Neha. Were you asking for me?'

'Oh! Good to see you, RG,' Rahul said, startled. 'You know, we've had this weird Japan experience . . .'

'I know all about it. Ghosts know everything that happens in the corridors they haunt.'

'But my question is: why is this happening to Neha and me? We're just visitors here.'

RG paused, sipped from his coffee mug (he never put it down) and narrated a story.

'Rahul and Neha, everything happens with a purpose in these parts. Saito, who brought the magical coffee beans to Coorg from Japan, lived here on the Edobetta estate which he had founded. He was here until a ripe old age. Local legend says that he lived to be one hundred and twenty-four years old, which is really long even by Japanese standards. He was content, exporting his coffee and meditating before a small golden statue of a smiling Buddha. He was kind to his workers, but he lived somewhat in seclusion. I guess that's how monks live. He drank like a fish though and I have happily been his beneficiary. Oh! How he loved rum, this old monk. And when he got drunk, he danced just like Elvis Presley. Let me tell you that story later. Now, before he died, he is rumoured to have revealed a secret, a dangerous but lucrative one, to his housekeeper. I think that's why all this is happening to you.'

'What sort of a secret? Do you know what it was?'

'No, Rahul. I've tried to find out, but only the housekeeper knows. He will only share it with the right people. Not with a ghost like me.'

'How are we the right people, RG? We're just random visitors from Mumbai.'

'Saito was, above all, a lover of coffee. When he was drunk on strong rum, he would only talk about all the coffees he had had in life, like how some men talk about all the women in their lives. He would go on and on about a great shogun of Japan, who was his coffee-drinking partner. He spoke about how the shogun and he would sit in a huge castle and taste the finest French roast coffees, strong and aromatic, and powerful brews. He told me that some of these fine coffees also came in from the Dutch settlements in Nagasaki as offerings in tribute to this powerful shogun. And then once, when he was very drunk, he revealed to me that he had with him a great treasure that had been given to him by this shogun. What it is he did not say. But he told me that he would leave this treasure behind to a person who had an extreme love of coffee. Now, I wonder, could that be you?'

'Well, I do have an extreme love of coffee, RG. You are quite right about that, but am I looking for a treasure left behind by a Japanese monk? Never crossed my mind.' And then, suddenly, Rahul's eyes sparkled. 'But, you know, it has crossed my mind now. Do you know who Saito's housekeeper was? Is he alive? Can Neha and I meet him?'

'Yes, I know the man,' replied RG with a smile. 'I know him very well indeed. He is old now, walks with a stoop and everyone in the town of Suntikoppa knows him. His name is H. Jerome Pandian.'

10

Let us take a sneak peek at H. Jerome Pandian before Rahul gets to him. Pandian, also known as Jerome Anna to his friends, family and colleagues, is now a sprightly ninety-eight-year-old and easily the oldest man in Suntikoppa. For fifty years of his life, he was a loyal housekeeper and trusted servant to Saito at Edobetta estate.

H. Jerome Pandian's most distinguishing feature sits on his broad, dark face—a magnificent twirled moustache that has been his pride and joy. While Pandian's hair now is a light grey befitting his advanced age, his moustache is jet black as though it belongs to someone much younger. Some people say that it is because of his native town of Madurai in nearby Tamil Nadu, which is widely known for men with handsome moustaches. Others say that he grew this moustache at the explicit request of his master, Saito, who associated such grand facial hair with samurais and Japanese men of high status. In fact, one of the photographs that hung on the walls of Saito's bungalow featured the grandly mustachioed Gaishi Nagaoka of the Japanese military. After his master passed away, Pandian had requested for this photograph, which he had long admired, to be hung on the walls of his own modest house.

Pandian's moustache must also have been nurtured by the copious amounts of coffee that he drank in Saito's bungalow for so many years. Perhaps the magical coffee that Saito had brought from Japan and grown here in Coorg had this wonderful fertilizing effect, in addition to all its other unusual effects that we are now familiar with. Pandian loved his coffee, which explains why Saito and he got along so well.

Pandian's favourite style of coffee was, however, neither Japanese-inspired nor borrowed from other nations. It was the south Indian filter kaapi, in which the thick, rich coffee decoction percolates through a brass or steel filter. As soon as this filtration happened, he mixed this fresh, aromatic decoction with thick, hot milk and two extra-large heaps of sugar, and drank the kaapi through the wet strands of his luxurious moustache. Not once did Pandian deviate from this morning coffee routine. He told his neighbours that this entire process gave him joy and peace of mind at the start of each day.

That day, Pandian was happily engaged in this coffee filtering morning routine when Rahul arrived unannounced at his wooden door, accompanied by Neha, and RG, who was hovering invisibly in the background. Rahul wasted no time in getting to the nub of the matter.

'My good man, are you H. Jerome Pandian, housekeeper to the late monk Saito?'

'Yes, I am, Ayya. Welcome to my humble abode. Who are you, Sir?'

'I am Rahul and this is my wife, Neha,' Rahul said. Neha kicked Rahul hard on his shin for mouthing this blatant marital lie with a flat face, but she did smile a little. Undeterred by the sharp pain, Rahul continued. 'I love coffee, Jerome Pandian. I love coffee very much. And I am told you may have with you the secret to a treasure that your master left behind when he died.'

Pandian did not flinch, not even a little. He just twirled his moustache and invited the couple to sit down. He believed in being hospitable first and discussing secrets later. He served them filter coffee in small steel tumblers. A froth of bubbles covered the surface of the coffee. Rahul could feel the lightness of the bubbles on his tongue before the heavy coffee poured in. He found the filter coffee more flavourful than the espresso, very rich and with mild bitter notes. Thankfully, it did not have the taste of chicory, which he knew was used in these parts along with coffee, because this was an additive he detested. He could see that Neha was also sipping her coffee with a lot of pleasure, looking into her tumbler and then looking up at all of them with her eyes wide open.

'What wonderful and delicious coffee! Thank you! I've never had something like this before. Made by your own hands, I presume,' said Neha. This sudden and loud praise was quite uncharacteristic of her. Maybe the love for coffee was getting to her too.

Pandian smiled and nodded. Then he responded to Rahul, in plain and good Indian English. 'Yes, Ayya, my master left a great secret with me. A most valuable but dangerous secret he told me on his deathbed. A secret that leads to a great treasure, which was given to him by a great man. But he told me, not once but twice, this was to be shared only with someone who had a hunger, longing and love for coffee. Also someone who knows the answer, which is the first key to this secret. There is an answer that I have to seek, before sharing anything at all.'

Rahul was quick to respond. 'I have an extreme love for coffee, and I think I may have the answer that you are seeking too. From all the signs I have seen, I think your master left this secret for me.'

Pandian listened and continued. 'Ayya, you are the very first person to meet me and ask about this treasure. I don't know how you know about this treasure, but you do know. And those who know a little about a big thing always have the hunger to know more, that's what we say. But there is a problem. I cannot share this secret with you, even if you give me the answer I seek.'

'Why not?' asked Rahul. 'What stops you, Pandian? You have a glorious moustache, and swearing on your moustache, I am a very big lover of coffee. That's why I am here in Coorg to begin with. I will meet all of your master's conditions.'

Pandian looked at him in a matter-of-fact way. 'Ayya, there is one condition you do not meet. My master, the monk, he said to me that this secret is to be revealed only to a woman. Not to a man. Men are strong, but they are always greedy for power. They may misuse this secret for power. But a woman, she is strong in a different way. She may be greedy for love and happiness, but not for power. She will use the secret well. So, my master told me a woman should answer the question, and she can then attempt to find this great treasure. Of course, there can be a man with her, to accompany her, as a servant or a companion or a guide. He mentioned that to me as well. My master was a man of detail, I know that, Ayya. I worked with him for fifty years.'

For the second time that morning, Neha jumped into the fray, unexpectedly and totally without forewarning. 'I am a woman, Pandian. I will answer your question and then you can reveal the secret to me. I will search for the treasure,' she said, 'Rahul here is my servant and obedient sidekick. He has been one for many months now. He wants to serve me in many ways, don't you, Rahul?'

Rahul gritted his teeth but Neha's response had excited him anyway. He answered using few words. 'Yes, Pandian, yes. I am her servant and companion. Neha will answer as she is a lover of coffee too. Didn't you see the way she slurped up your wonderful filter coffee?'

RG, who was invisible to everyone all this while, came up to Rahul and Neha and patted them on their shoulders. Both of them were taken by surprise at this; Neha even jumped up a little.

Pandian looked one way and then the other way. He went up to an old sepia photograph of a Japanese monk in robes, hanging on the wall, next to the picture of a man with the grand moustache.

'Master, I think the time has come. You spoke so correctly. You told me that a young couple would come to my house and ask for the secret. They are here, master. Guide me, shall I go ahead?'

RG, who was still hovering invisibly, decided to respond in his master's voice. 'Yes, Pandian, yes, yes,' he spoke from nowhere in a high-pitched, Japanese-sounding voice. Clearly, he remembered Saito's accent quite well. 'These are the chosen people. Please go ahead, Pandian. I am now going back into my silence. I am dead, I must rest.'

Pandian bowed, offered a prayer and went into his bedroom. He picked up a small, coffee-brown leather briefcase from under his cot. He looked at the briefcase fondly and dusted it carefully. And then he took it out to the living room where Neha, Rahul and RG waited expectantly.

'So now, I will open this bag for you. It belonged to my master. "Tell them to look, tell them to observe, tell them to think, for not everything will be clear, except to the right people who are worthy of this secret" were his words.'

'Wait, wait,' said Neha, taking charge of the conversation. 'Wait, Pandian. Tell me, what should we look for? How long can we look? Don't rush to open this stuff before you tell us everything.'

'Amma, this is a bag that my master packed with his own hands just a few days before he died. It contains many things which were precious to him. How do I know what you should look for, when I myself have never opened this bag? You should look, you should observe and you should think. That's all I know.'

With this, Pandian placed the bag on a tall wooden stool. It looked very old, with thin cracks visible on the brown leather which had a very seasoned look. Rahul stepped closer, he felt the leather gently and smelt it. He trusted his sense of smell more than his other senses because he firmly believed that smell, unlike the other senses, never lets anyone down. The leather smelt faintly of the coffee plantations, but it also had a distant whiff of the cemetery in Tokyo.

And then, with a flourish worthy of a performing magician, Pandian threw open the bag.

11

Pandian, the custodian and opener of the bag, stepped aside reverentially as soon as he opened it. Then he looked into the bag, scanned its contents silently and stood still. His face betrayed no emotion, nothing at all.

Rahul, lover of coffee and obedient servant of Neha, took two steps forward immediately. He did not want to waste even a minute, lest the bag shut firmly again because you never knew what the monk had ordained. He touched the bag, ran his hands over the pouches inside it and then retracted.

Neha, the recently declared treasure hunter with a newly discovered love of coffee, went up, bent her head and smelt the bag. The dusty, musty smell of the bag that had just been opened after several years assailed her nostrils. She looked at Rahul as if to silently ask what was next.

RG, invisible to everyone, floated around the bag and poked its contents gently. He knew what was coming up. It was a puzzle, a clue to the great treasure. He remembered what the monk had told him not once, but twice. This wonderful monk had loved puzzles, particularly when he was a trifle drunk on his favourite rum.

'This is a puzzle. This will be exciting, so go on,' he whispered to Rahul and Neha.

Let's look into the bag now, the place where the secret rested for so many years. Seven small pouches, all identical, made of brown cloth, jute maybe. Each pouch carried markings in Japanese, a character of the Japanese alphabet, written in beautiful, broad, black brush strokes. The mouth of each pouch was closed with a slender, red silk rope. Intertwined with this rope, in each case, was a small card, with some writing on it. On the inside cover of the briefcase, which faced them now, were two words written in capital alphabets: TAKE ONE.

Neha and Rahul looked at each other. 'What shall we do? Take one pouch, it says. Which one, Rahul?'

Rahul felt a couple of the pouches with his thumb and forefinger. He instantly knew what they contained. *Of course*, he told himself, *what else could they contain.*

'Neha, these pouches have coffee beans in them. Coffee beans packed by the monk himself. Let's think carefully.'

'Think. Think. Both of you think. This is a big treasure, don't miss it,' said RG. He sipped his mug of coffee and started thinking too.

Suddenly, there was too much thinking going on in the room, that too all at once. If there was a measure for the amount of thinking, like kilograms or metres or something similar, then we would have noted the quantum of thought to be almost explosive.

71

In the absence of such a metric, Neha decided to rely on her instincts.

'Stop, Rahul. This is coffee, you know it well. What is the first thing we do with coffee?'

'We drink it.'

'No, no. Even before we drink it, what do we do?'

'We brew the coffee.'

'No, that's not what I meant. What do you do first, when a cup of hot coffee is given to you?'

'Oh, I smell the coffee. Inhale deeply and savour its aroma. That's what I do.'

'So, let's follow our nose, Rahul. Let's smell these pouches. I think that's how we will be able to choose one.'

'Good thought, Neha. You are the sniffer. You lead the way.'

'Go ahead, Neha,' RG said encouragingly.

Neha picked up the first pouch, loosened the red rope to create an opening, stuck her nose in and smelt the beans. The smell came as a sharp whiff and she felt a sense of relaxation seep into her. She suddenly remembered a news item she had recently read, according to which the aroma of coffee beans helped relieve stress caused by sleep deprivation and lack of sexual activity.

She picked up the second pouch. Here, there was a distinctive smell of jackfruit. Yes, this was coffee grown in the hinterland of jackfruit trees. There are a lot of jackfruits in these parts, loved by the elephants.

Neha then moved to the third pouch. She had to smell these beans twice before she could make out the aroma—a hint of pepper and, again, warm mustiness. Coffee intergrown with pepper vines.

But it was on the fourth pouch that Neha struck gold. As soon as she put her nose in, she smelt the nutty aromas that both of them had encountered so often over the past few days. A deep, walnutty aroma that went straight into the depths of her nose and reminded her of the old woman and the pink beans, the fuzzy coffee cups on the verandah on the bungalow, and, most recently, the mysterious happenings in Mayaso Coffee Shop in Tokyo.

Neha, the expert sniffer and olfactory genius, had found the pouch of coffee that they had to pick. She took a small jump, did a spontaneous waltz and held up the pouch.

'Rahul, I have it here. Right here, right here.'

'How did you make it out?'

'This has the wonderful aroma of walnut. The same smell that has followed us everywhere. That's why it has followed us. This is what we were meant to find.'

She handed over the pouch to Rahul. He smelt it too. Yes, of course! Yes, yes, yes! This was it. He felt the jute; it was soft and firm. Then, he saw the card attached to the pouch and began reading the words written on it. Words written with turquoise-blue ink in very precise calligraphic script:

Three shrines of coffee have I now foreseen, three Goddesses that nurture our love for the bean. From river to ocean, each shows you the way. Find me these shrines, and then will I say: Here's my treasure, let it fill up your day.

He first read it to himself and then loudly. *What could this rhyme possibly mean?* Clearly, it was some sort of a puzzle. What exactly are shrines of coffee, and who are these goddesses? How would these shrines show them the way to this treasure? To begin with, how would they find these shrines? Where in the world would they go? What was the great treasure that the coffee monk Saito had left behind?

Finally, Pandian spoke. He added a formal note by giving his grand moustache a twirl. 'Ayya, Amma, you can take the card and the pouch you have selected. My master had instructed me to tell you that. Take it with you, the blessings of my master are with you. Oh, and by the way, I should not forget. He asked me to tell you two things after you have selected the pouch. One, you should know that coffee was his first love. He believed that coffee could change the world. He also asked me to tell you that India was his second big love. He loved our people, he travelled a lot across our country and when he lived here he brought great happiness to the coffee plantations all around. I hope you fulfil what he had in mind and I hope you find his treasure. Ayya, Amma, vanakkam.'

Exactly at that point, they heard a commotion erupt outside Pandian's front door. They could hear fists banging hard on the door. Rahul listened but he could not understand the language, even as the shouting, screaming and banging were clearly audible. Once again, before anyone could react, there were loud knocks. It was evident that the old wooden door would collapse under this sudden and rather vicious attack.

Pandian walked up to the door and threw it open. Outside stood three local villagers, amongst them there was Krishnappa, a burly man from the immediate neighbourhood. He spoke, 'Who is this strange ruffian, Pandian? Do you know him? He says he will destroy the houses in this town if his treasure is not given to him. He says that there is a stolen treasure in your house and bad people are now searching for it. Your house of all places? Is he mad? Where has he come from, this fancy dress idiot?'

He pointed to a totally bald man with spectacles standing a short distance away. The man was wearing some sort of a strange, short, blue gown, tied at the waist with a red cloth band. He was also wearing a blue headband. On his chest was a long necklace with a large, square-shaped wooden pendant. He was surrounded by a few villagers who were determined to pin him down. Astonishingly, he held a sword in one hand.

Krishnappa went on, 'He came from nowhere, running down our main road with this ridiculous sword. He spoke in poor, slow English, but we understood what he said. And then, he threatened us by running up and down, waving his sword, and it became clear that he wanted to break into your house. Do you know him, Pandian? Is he a relative of that yellow monk you served on the plantation? What audacity does this man have to come to our village and threaten all of us?'

Pandian looked hard, but he had never seen this man before. A few strange visitors from Japan had come to his master's bungalow over the years when the monk was alive, but not this man. None bearing a sword. He gulped and said nothing.

Then Neha spoke, 'Rahul, I know who that is. That is one of the Yamamoto brothers. One of the two guys who took us to that strange graveyard in Tokyo. It surely looks like him!'

Rahul looked closely and, yes, it was him! It was the man who had introduced himself as Takahira Yamamoto in the Mayaso Coffee Shop. What was he doing here in this small village in India? What sort of a dangerous mess had they got themselves into?

*

It was indeed Takahira Yamamoto, the man from Tokyo. Though he was surrounded by at least twenty villagers, he was entirely unfazed. He stared back at them, silently and sullenly. Then, in a dramatic gesture, he brandished his sword, held it high above his head and spun it around two times. This was mainly for effect because the circle of people appeared to be closing in on him. The villagers, alarmed by this unannounced swinging of the sword, retreated a little but continued to surround him, this time in a more spread out circle. They would not let this mad man from somewhere, who knows where, run amok all over their village.

Takahira looked out beyond the circle of villagers. His gaze stopped at Rahul and Neha, who were standing at the door of Pandian's house. It was the young man and woman he had first met at Mayaso, as instructed. He had tracked them down successfully to this village, to this very house. *Takahira, you are on the right track. This young man and woman have been brought to my brother and me by destiny. I am blessed by the spirits themselves. I will follow them, my dear beloved Father, and I will find what I need to find.*

From within his garment, he took out a small cloth pouch. He inhaled deeply from it. The gentle aroma of summer coffee, an aroma originally sourced from Mayaso Coffee Shop, swam into his head. It was the same aroma that had shown him the way here in the first place. He put his sword back in his sheath. He bowed deep to the villagers who were surrounding him. 'I go back to my place now as I find what I came for,' he said to them in slow and broken English. And then, very quietly, he briskly walked through the startled circle of villagers, right down the end of the main road of Suntikoppa. Before Rahul, Neha or anyone else could react, he got into a waiting car, a smart orange Tata Nexon, and quietly drove away.

12

Still standing in Pandian's house, with the selected pouch of coffee beans in his hand, Rahul was perplexed by this sudden turn of events. He was also concerned about this bald Japanese man who had randomly appeared and then disappeared. *Why was Takahira Yamamoto stalking them? Had he put his own life, and Neha's too, in danger by impulsively coming out to Pandian's house in search of some unknown treasure that may have no meaning for them at all? Should they return to Mumbai immediately, happy with their truncated holiday, and put this entirely unnecessary adventure safely behind them?*

'Pandian, too much is happening here, and too fast. I need to sit down and think. Can you give us a nice cup of coffee?'

Pandian was delighted to fulfil the request. He took the greatest possible pride in his coffee. He was a master in the art of making south Indian filter coffee, one he had perfected while working with the monk on Edobetta plantation for over four decades. 'Ayya, I will make you the finest kaapi you have ever tasted. Give me just ten minutes.'

He took out his old brass filter from a cupboard in his kitchen. The filter was given to him by his father, and he used it only on very special occasions. This metal device consisted of two cylinders, one placed on top of another. The top cylinder was pierced at the bottom and resembled a sieve. This cylinder also held a sort of pressing disc with a long, flat brass handle.

Pandian then opened a tin box that held fresh coffee powder. The aroma immediately wafted through the room. It was magnificent, full of warm notes that suffused the air and stimulated the senses beautifully and instantly. It was so enthralling that Neha took a deep breath to capture and lock the aromas deep within her lungs.

These aromas developed during the roasting process, which Pandian carried out carefully on an iron pan placed on the wood stove in his own home. These days very few people had the patience and skill to roast their own coffee beans at home, but Pandian insisted. He had learnt from the monk that careful roasting of beans helps develop over 800 different and delicious aroma compounds that blend together to offer a beautiful cup of coffee. He knew that dark roasting, for its deep and slightly burnt flavour, was best suited for the strong south Indian kaapi that he loved. He was also aware of the exact temperature and duration which gave it the perfect roast. For him, it had always been a labour of love, the roasting.

He carefully put six teaspoons of these roasted ground beans into the top cylinder of the filter, squeezed the disc down, twisted it a little, affixed this cylinder to the bottom one and added boiling water to the brim in the top cylinder. Then, he put a lid on top. Slowly, over the next few minutes, the brewed coffee decoction would drip into the bottom cylinder in the form of dense, brown drops of strong, concentrated coffee. This decoction was typically stronger than the Italian espresso, but unlike the espresso which was always drunk in a black dollop, it would usually be consumed only after adding hot milk and sugar. It has, in fact, been described as the nectar of Coorg.

'Ayya, this coffee comes from the plantation next to this town, Suntikoppa estate. Actually, our town takes its name from this estate. This coffee is special because it grows in an estate that is home to three beautiful birds: the Malabar grey hornbill, the spotted dove and the drongo. They are our own birds and they look after this coffee for us.'

Pandian now detached the lower cylinder. Rahul and Neha could see that the strong, black coffee decoction had now filled up nearly to the brim. Once again, the heavenly whiff of smoky, malty, vanilla-like coffee floated all around them in a delicious haze.

'How much sugar should I add, Ayya and Amma?' asked Pandian. They requested a spoon each. Both Rahul and Neha liked a tinge of sweetness, but not to a point where it overwhelmed the bitterness of the coffee. The sweet and bitter flavours had to sit in balance with each other for a perfect cup.

They heard a whisper in their ears. RG again was ensuring that his presence was not forgotten. 'Drink the coffee. Savour the coffee. Pandian's coffee is the best there is here. I can still feel it on my tongue even after so many years. It will give you the answers, oh yes, it will.'

They sat down on the sofa chairs and sipped the coffee. Pandian, now the coffee master, kept standing and observing their expressions closely. In the first sip, Rahul felt the smooth, thick coffee roll over his tongue, the milk and sugar in a wonderful medley with the bitter coffee brew. He thought to himself, this first sip is even more beautiful than the first hint of an orgasm that is unstoppably on its way. He didn't know why that random thought occurred to him just then, but it did. He looked at Neha, who was enjoying her own coffee, and realized that this comparison was foolish and incorrect. Nothing, not even the best coffee in the world, could remotely match up to making love to her. *And I know why*, he told himself. It struck him then that this was no time for such leisurely musings; they had more urgent things at hand.

A couple of sips of good coffee always had the effect of making him think. He held up the pouch and read the card once again:

Three shrines of coffee have I now foreseen, three goddesses
that nurture our love for the bean. From river to ocean, each
shows you the way. Find me these shrines, and then will I say:
Here's my treasure, let it fill up your day.

With the warm filter coffee surging through his gut, he found that all his earlier doubts and hesitation about the danger they were facing were melting away.

'Neha, this is our own exciting adventure. Let's not quit now. Who knows when something like this will happen again in our lives? Let's go after the treasure, whatever and wherever it is. I think we are destined to be the finders of this treasure. Why else would all these things be suddenly happening to us? Let's not worry about bald Japanese men and other aimless distractions. They will come and go. Come on, let's move and solve this puzzle. This is about coffee and we love coffee, don't we? Are you with me, Neha?'

Rahul looked at Neha and held her hand. The coffee-induced pleasure was visible in her eyes. She looked back at him and squeezed his hand. 'Yes, Rahul. Count me in.'

RG tapped Rahul gently on the shoulder. 'Count me in too,' he said.

*

They thanked Pandian and left his house with the pouch of old coffee beans and the card attached to it. Rahul added as they left, 'Pandian, your filter coffee was the best. Even if we don't find your master's treasure, the memory and taste of your coffee is a treasure we are taking with us. What a medley of rich flavours you have created in a single cup, my dear friend. God be with you.'

After they left, Pandian bowed to a framed photograph of his master, the Japanese monk Saito. 'Master, I have finally finished the big task you left me so many years ago. Thank you, master, for bringing these young people to my humble abode before I breathe my last. I pray that they find the big treasure of coffee which you have left behind. I pray for them because I think they love coffee very much, just like you and me. Both the young man and the woman, how they enjoyed my little cup of filter coffee. I hope they will be back here soon.'

The young man and the woman, meanwhile, were poring over the card attached to the pouch. They were back at Cottabetta, seated on the verandah. How in this big, wide world would they find the three shrines where the secrets to the monk's treasure were possibly hidden?

'I think we should start in Japan,' Rahul concluded after some time. 'That's where the monk was from. That's where that last shogun was from, whom this monk knew well. Maybe there is a shrine there, built for a goddess of coffee or someone like that? I have heard that the Japanese have gods for everything. It could even be a shrine that the shogun or the monk established. This is one of the four shrines mentioned in this old note. At least one man in Japan, our bald friend Takahira Yamamoto, appears quite interested in what we are doing. What do you think, Neha?'

Neha was now increasingly excited by the possibilities of where this adventure could take them. She was bitten by the travel bug, though the recent, and rather unconventional, visit to Tokyo had shaken her up a little bit. She would journey on aircrafts, trains or even boats if necessary. Pink coffee-induced magical journeys were not her preferred mode of global travel. But as she listened to Rahul, Japan did not quite sound right to her.

'I don't think so, Rahul. Even that bald Japanese guy, he came all the way to India. I think the shrines are out here in India and not in Japan. Here is where the monk lived for fifty long years. You heard what Pandian said. He loved this country. India was his second love after coffee. That's what my instinct tells me.'

Rahul nodded. 'Good thinking, Neha. It's been a long day. Let's talk about this tomorrow. For now, I know where my instincts are leading me. Somewhere very special, and I have something equally adventurous planned for the evening. Just you and me.' He smiled.

*

When they returned to their room at Cottabetta Bungalow, Rahul requested Neha to sit on the verandah and watch the darkening skies for a bit, even as he prepared their room for the night. 'It's a surprise for you. Actually, for both of us.'

Fifteen minutes later, he turned up next to her. Neha could smell freshly roasted coffee all over his hands and body. Rahul and his extreme love of coffee. *Had he brewed a cup of something special for her?*

Indeed he had, but it was not the usual. He led her to the room and threw open the thick teak doors with a flourish. Inside, there was muted bedside lighting. Neha's eyes went to the bed. Scattered on their four-poster bed were roasted coffee beans, lots and lots of them. They formed a dark brown carpet across the firm, thick mattress, evenly spread out. The oil that coated the roasted beans was glistening in the mellow light like some surreal surface.

'I have read that coffee is a great aphrodisiac, Neha. It stimulates and elevates us every day. Many cultures across the world know that it also enhances stamina. So, will you have coffee with me tonight?'

Neha smiled coyly at him, a teasing smile that always made him go weak in the knees and everywhere else. Within a moment, they had turned off the lights. The coffee smelt and tasted and felt even more delicious than before. It was pure, washed arabica, love roasted to perfection.

PART B

THE SEARCH

13

Three shrines of coffee have I now foreseen, three goddesses
that nurture our love for the bean. From river to ocean, each
shows you the way. Find me these shrines, and then will I say:
Here's my treasure, let it fill up your day.

Rahul read the lines aloud to Neha for the tenth time that
morning. What did they actually mean? Both of them looked at
each other silently and acknowledged that they were stumped.
Totally clueless.

Outside, dawn had broken and they could hear the high-
pitched charr-charr notes of a single woodpecker breaking the
stark silence of the coffee plantations around them. Inside, most
of the coffee beans had fallen off the bed and were strewn all over
the floor. It had been a memorable night and now they knew for
sure that coffee was a great stimulant.

But where was the stimulant that would help them figure out
this puzzle, one written by a mysterious monk who had died long
ago, leaving a great treasure hidden? Where were these three shrines
that the monk had spoken of? Where exactly should they begin?

Pooviah brought them their morning coffee in an elegant tray with a pot and two cups of white bone china. 'Sir, I used those pink coffee beans you gave me to make coffee for Madam and for you today. The smell of this coffee is getting better with each passing day, Sir.'

The old woman's coffee! In the midst of all the other excitements of the past two days, Rahul had nearly forgotten about this. 'Yes, yes, Pooviah, please pour coffee for us.'

The walnutty flavour came back to them once again. Superb! As they sipped the coffee, Neha leant back and read the puzzle once again. Suddenly, she could clearly see the author himself, the venerable monk. He appeared vividly in her mind. Orange-robed monk, fat, bald and peaceful, walking somewhere. Where was he walking to? And then, behind the monk, she saw flowing waters. A few words from the puzzle swam in front of her now-dilated pupils: *From river to ocean, each shows you the way*.

She sat up with a start. 'Rahul, listen. Listen to me. We need to go to a river, one that will show us the way to the first shrine. That's what the monk meant when he wrote "from river to ocean". The river first, and then the ocean will show us the way. That's why he put those words in his note, to give us a clue. I can see him in my mind, Rahul. He is walking by that river, right over there, right now.'

Rahul glanced at the lines once again. What Neha said made sense. They had nothing else to go on anyway. Then, he remembered something, a local guidebook kept in their room that he had briefly gone over yesterday. It spoke of a river nearby.

He went into the room, brought out the small guidebook, turned a few pages, and began reading aloud:

> The Kaveri is the patron goddess of all coffee growers in Coorg. Flowing through the beautiful coffee plantations and nurturing them like her own special children, the Kaveri is the great river of this region. Originating in the foothills of the Western Ghats, the river meanders through the region of Coorg and the vast Deccan plateau before it eventually flows into the Bay of Bengal. The Kaveri quenches this region's thirst for water and makes it one of the most fertile lands known to mankind. From these lands of the Kaveri come some of the finest coffees the world has ever known.

Rahul turned to Neha. 'Neha, I think you are absolutely right. We must go to the Kaveri. That's where we will begin.'

He continued reading the guidebook.

> The Kaveri is not merely a river, but a goddess who is worshipped by everyone in this coffee growing region of Coorg. The unique coffee of Coorg springs from the sweet waters of this sacred river. Coffee requires a lot of water for its flowering, and the Kaveri provides it in abundance. The varieties of coffee grown on the fertile banks of the Kaveri are known for their robust body, light acidity and soft liquor, making them some of the most sought-after beans in the world.

Rahul paused here, absorbing this beautiful description of the coffee. 'Robust body, light acidity, soft liquor, wow! I must taste these coffees from the banks of the Kaveri.' Then he saw something in the guidebook which made his pulse quicken. He read it out in hushed tones:

> There are many shrines built for the Kaveri, to worship and celebrate this goddess, who is the presiding deity of the region. The best known shrine is located at the source of the river called Talakaveri. The river originates near this shrine, as a spring, and the water then flow underground to emerge as the magnificent Kaveri some distance away. The road to Talakaveri is surrounded by coffee plantations and suffused by the intoxicating aromas of coffee. Many monks and holy people visit this shrine throughout the year.

Rahul turned to Neha. 'We must go to Talakaveri, Neha. I am sure that is where our Japanese monk has left directions for us. He must have visited this shrine and left something there. This is a shrine of the river that nurtures coffee, and so it is a shrine of coffee itself. That is what the monk must have meant. This is where our search must begin.'

Neha nodded quickly. Yes, this appeared right instinctively. She took the guidebook away from Rahul's hands and quickly read it once more. 'Yes, let's go, Rahul. Right now.'

RG, who was a witness to this guidebook-led conversation, smiled. This was the moment he had been waiting for all through his afterlife. He tapped Rahul lightly and said, 'I am coming with you, Rahul. It has been a long, long time since I saw the Talakaveri shrine. I am coming too.'

The Search

Unknown to Rahul and Neha, at that very moment, one other person was deeply interested in what they planned to do. Takahira Yamamoto was slowly walking down the streets of a nearby village. He was getting impatient. When would these two young people begin their search? He had to find what he had come here for. His shining, sharp sword was ready. He would not let anything, anything at all, come in his way.

14

Rahul and Neha, accompanied by a happy RG, set out to Talakaveri in a jeep. It was a long drive and their first stop for refreshments was at Gonikoppal, the same village where they had acquired the pink coffee beans. They looked around for the old lady, but she was nowhere to be seen.

As their jeep approached Talakaveri, they saw lush green hills unfolding before them, rolling over into each other like carpets. These were the Brahmagiri hills, their driver informed them. 'That is where the sacred men go to meditate,' he said, 'I have been there just once, with my friends. It is a difficult climb to the top, Ayya.'

When they finally reached Talakaveri, the town which housed the shrine of Goddess Kaveri, they paused. Here she was, the river goddess whose blessings nurtured the splendid coffees of Coorg. Her shrine, just ahead of them, was by the hillside, and it was thronged by people.

Then, a question (which has presumably accosted several adventurers over the ages) occurred to Rahul. They had reached what was ostensibly the first shrine. So far, so good. But now what? What were they supposed to do next?

RG answered that question even before he was asked. He poked Rahul on his shoulder, pointed to the hill that was right in front of them and said in a loud voice that even Neha could hear, 'That monk often spoke about how he meditated on top of a hill and found some wonderful coffee there. He said it was the hill of the gods. I think our next steps are clear.'

They began climbing the steps hewn into the hillside. There was lush green vegetation all around, a bright blue sky above and the smell of the earth below them. There were a couple of shops selling coffee and honey along the path.

On an impulse, Rahul held Neha's hand and raced up a few steps. Stopping for breath at a clearing, they looked up at the skies and saw a few birds flying in perfect formation, heading somewhere with great purpose. Neha turned to Rahul and said wistfully, 'Look at those birds, they know their way for sure. I wonder where we are going, Rahul, and how we will get there.'

Not knowing how to respond, Rahul squeezed her hand tighter. He was excellent when it came to writing emotive advertising scripts, but expressing himself in his personal life did not come as easily. They were still a few steps away from the top of the hill when they saw a small, beautiful idol on a platform. It was an idol of a voluptuous woman with a pot of water in her hands. 'That's Goddess Kaveri.' Rahul recognized her from his guidebook. 'See, she is carrying the brass pot which has the river within it!' The idol seemed to draw them towards itself, so they went closer and looked around. And then Neha burst out in excitement.

'Rahul, see this! See this now! This is absolutely the first shrine.'

'What's the excitement, Neha? I know this is the shrine, because this is the goddess. That's what I just said.'

'Look at the base of this platform, Rahul. It has markings in Chinese or Japanese, I can't figure out which. Clearly, our monk was here!'

Rahul looked and, sure enough, there was a line of Japanese script etched into the base of the platform. He was clueless as to what it meant, but it sure was a sign. Yes, the monk had come here to meditate and had left this sign behind.

'Brilliant, Neha. It's clear. This is a shrine where our monk had been. This is where we begin our quest. The monk's puzzle says that each shrine will tell us the way to the next one.'

They walked around the idol a few times. Neha felt the limbs of the idol, looking closely for any more markings, but there were none. Rahul knocked at various points of the idol, wondering if there was a hollow space where the monk may have left something. He too found nothing. They peered into the brass pot which the goddess held, a space where it would have been easy to leave something hidden. But that was empty too.

They tapped the earth beneath the idol, brushing away a few stones to see if they could spot anything below the grass, but this too came to naught. Should they now search for something buried in the earth? They would need help for that. Maybe their driver, Kaverappa, could get some locals.

At precisely that moment, a young man came up to them and spoke in halting English.

'Sir, Madam? Are you looking for something, from a Buddhist monk perhaps? I think I can help you if you are the people I have been waiting for. I have a small coffee shop just opposite the road. Come, walk with me.'

The man led them to his shop. Rahul spoke, 'Yes, we are looking for something that a monk left behind. Why do you think you can help us?'

The young man responded immediately. 'Sir, I will tell you very soon. My name is Venkatesha. I have a secret to share, and I think this secret is from Japan. But first, you are my guests. Let me make you some of my special bellada kaapi.'

*

Bellada kaapi. Loosely translated it means coffee with jaggery. But this translation does not capture the uniqueness of this beverage which is so delicious and heavenly; it may very well have been the preferred drink of Goddess Kaveri herself.

Bellada kaapi. The drink that Venkatesha was now preparing for his guests using a secret recipe handed down generation after generation. Later, he would reveal to his guests another secret, one handed down to him by his father. But that was later.

For now, the aroma of fresh filter coffee filled the little coffee shop with its old rosewood benches that wore a polished look, thanks to the millions of weary backsides that had sat eagerly and lazily on them for years and years, awaiting their favourite cup of bellada kaapi.

Venkatesha brewed the decoction first in his brass filter. 'I use only the finest robusta coffee beans from the nearby Cannoncadoo estate,' he announced. 'And do you know why? This coffee shop you are sitting in is at Talakaveri, the source of the Kaveri. And the most beautiful, sweet and quiet streams of this river flow through Cannoncadoo estate. It is one of the few coffee plantations here that is located directly on the banks of the river. That unique location produces a coffee of marvellous taste, so soft and smooth, perfect for bellada kaapi, which has been the signature drink at my family's coffee shop for generations!'

Then, he brought the milk to a boil on his stove and added jaggery powder to it. The fresh jaggery blended into the milk, sweetening it slowly and adding a touch of golden brown. In the air around them, the light, sweet smell of jaggery milk mingled nicely with the strong, dark aroma of the robusta coffee decoction.

Venkatesha poured the coffee decoction into steel tumblers. He added the jaggery sweetened milk into each tumbler and mixed it well. He offered Rahul and Neha a cup each, and RG, invisible in the background, felt deprived.

Bellada kaapi. Beautiful, warm, jaggery coffee that ran down Rahul and Neha's throats, creating sensations that they never knew could exist. Sweet, soft, strong, stimulating, delicious and extraordinary, this was probably the best coffee yet to be discovered by the rest of the world. It could well become a global rage, much like the famous PSL (pumpkin spice latte) or even the flat white. The warm drink had calmed them down. They instantly relaxed and their hands brushed lightly against each other, their eyes stealing fleeting glances quite deliberately, even as they waited for Venkatesha to reveal his other secret, the one they were here for.

Then Venkatesha began his story.

'Sir and Madam, this coffee shop makes the best bellada kaapi in the world. My grandfather, Srinivasa, founded this shop exactly seventy years ago. He invented the recipe for the coffee that you are drinking right now. The exact origin and type of jaggery used, the robusta coffee from Cannoncaddoo estate, roasted to my grandfather's precise specifications, those are the secrets behind this fabulous flavour and taste. He died only seven years after this shop opened and my father, who is known in these parts as Bellada Kaapi Raghavendra, took over.

'This coffee shop soon started drawing people from far and near. They spoke about the coffee to their friends and word spread quickly. Pilgrims who came to Talakaveri temple also became frequent pilgrims to Bellada Kaapi Raghavendra's Coffee Shop. This shop virtually became a shrine of coffee. My father prospered. As a token of thanksgiving, he installed the idol of Goddess Kaveri in front of the shop, where you were searching just now. Every morning, he offered prayers before this sacred idol, to thank the river that gave birth to this wonderful coffee and jaggery that have made our shop so successful.'

Rahul sat up with a start, when he heard the words 'shrine of coffee'. He wondered if the monk had borrowed those exact words from here.

'Then, one day, a very different sort of man came to our coffee shop. He was dressed in the pale orange robes of a monk. He was elderly, maybe more than eighty years old, with wrinkles showing on his face and a totally bald head, like some monks prefer. I was a very small boy then, but I still remember him clearly. He told my father that he was from Japan but had settled down on a coffee plantation nearby. He drank cup after cup of bellada kaapi, as if his thirst for coffee could never be quenched. He had a long discussion with my father, for over two hours, about coffee and jaggery, various types of coffee beans and how many unique types of coffee brews there are in countries across the world. He had come across over eight thousand unique types of coffee preparations, he said. My father was very interested.

'The monk came to our coffee shop quite often over the next few years. He said he came to this hill to meditate, and that our bellada kaapi was a wonderful way to conclude his meditation. Each time, my father and he would sit down and discuss coffee endlessly. Eight thousand different types of coffee can generate lots and lots of interesting conversation. Then, on one of his last visits, the monk made a strange request, which my father accepted immediately because he liked this man a lot and admired his vast knowledge.

'He gave my father a cloth pouch containing coffee beans and a sealed envelope. He said this envelope contained a secret which led to a great treasure, and that we should never open it. He requested my father to keep these safe. He said someone would come searching for them in the distant future. He also told us that we would see these people searching near the idol of the Goddess Kaveri, the very same idol that my father had installed. He wrote something at the base of this idol using a sharp knife to chisel the words. He said this was a Japanese prayer that would bring continued prosperity to our small shop. And here you are, Sir, here you are. My father is now very old and does not come to the shop any more. But he asked me to look out for the monk's promised people, every single day. This is a blessing for me, Sir, to see you here today.'

*

Venkatesha went to a shelf at the back of the coffee shop and pulled out an old tin. He opened it and took out a cloth pouch and an old brown envelope. He handed these over to Rahul.

Rahul held up the envelope to the light. It had aged considerably and had a marked musty smell to it. He smelt the coffee beans, breathing in the familiar nutty, walnutty smell. The envelope had a couple of lines written on top of it:

> The first shrine of coffee you have now found. The bellada kaapi here can make the world go round. Now to the second shrine and treasure, starting today. Within this envelope, I will point you the way.

Clearly, the monk loved his rhymes as much as he loved his coffee—and, not to forget, his rum.

Rahul turned to Venkatesha. 'Thank you, Venkatesha. That bellada kaapi was extraordinary. What beautiful coffees exist here, ones we never knew about. And thanks for telling us this story and giving us this envelope. We will take it to our bungalow at Cottabetta and read what is inside it at leisure.'

Rahul was eager to open the envelope right away, but he did not want Venkatesha or anyone else in the coffee shop to see what was written inside.

*

Not far away, seated at the base of a tree on Brahmagiri Hill, Takahira Yamamoto was peering at them through his high-powered Toshiba 100x ultrazoom binoculars. He had a thin smile on his face, a satisfied smirk that said nothing but revealed everything. He had keenly observed the long conversation between the young man and Rahul, he saw them drinking coffee together, and then he sat up as he saw the brown envelope being handed over.

Takahira, you're on the right track with this young couple. This is about your treasure, Takahira. Your family's treasure. It was stolen unfairly, brazenly, by that wretched coffee monk. Now, you will get it back.

*

Rahul and Neha left the coffee shop with the envelope tucked away in Rahul's trouser pocket and the cloth pouch in Neha's handbag. Before they went down the hill to their car, they stopped at the idol of Goddess Kaveri one last time. The goddess' face was captivating and her full lips held a gentle smile. Neha thought she could suddenly see a twinkle in her eyes. The goddess of coffee was wishing them Godspeed.

15

Back in their bungalow at Cottabetta, Rahul kept aside the bag of coffee beans after smelling it deeply once more. There was no mistaking the nutty aroma. Then, he opened the monk's envelope. There was a single sheet of paper inside, with the same handwriting. It was just two brief lines:

In our own splendid Manchester lives the goddess of food.
Her shrine is a temple of coffee.

By now, Neha was beginning to like the monk and his penchant for puzzles. And she definitely liked the direction this clue seemed to be pointing to.

'This is a good one, Rahul,' she piped up, 'and what's really exciting is that this clue could take us all the way to England and Manchester! The land of the Beatles; we may even meet Elton John!'

Rahul sat back. First, a graveyard in Japan and now a shrine in England. He hoped the monk's treasure, when they found it that is, was worth all these journeys. On the other hand, just the opportunity to travel with Neha to all these places was well worth the while. She appeared keen, so he wasn't complaining.

In any case, Haroon had given him a month off to do whatever he wanted. After the enthusiastic acceptance of the Nippon Springlove advertisement by the client, and the windfall it was now promising to bring them, he deserved that much time and space, Haroon had said.

'Well, Neha, this one is definitely pointing towards England. But first, let's do some research on Manchester. I have never come across an English goddess of food, unless our good monk is referring to Nigella Lawson. Nigella does have a goddess sort of figure, but I don't think Manchester has built a shrine for her yet. Or maybe they have, who knows? Anything can happen, these days. Let's take a quick look.'

Over a few cups of coffee, they googled virtually everything about Manchester, from shrines to goddesses and temples of coffee. Manchester, after all, is the highest-ranked city in England after London, with its rich history of industry and warehouses. It is also home to two of the finest football clubs in Europe. Who hasn't heard of Manchester United and Manchester City?

'Look at this, Rahul. Look at the number of craft coffee shops that have taken over Manchester. All of them are independent stores serving great coffee. No wonder the monk wants us to go there. Here's one called Fig and Sparrow. What a wonderful name, very British. Talks about their flat white coffees. And here's another nice one—Grindsmith. Tiny shop, if you judge by the photograph, but the reviews say it serves flawless coffee. Ancoats Coffee Company, which specializes in exotic single-origin brews.

Just a small walk from their original coffee roastery. Wow, the whole of Manchester appears to be a temple of coffee.

'But what about the goddess of food and her shrine, Rahul? There are no references to that anywhere.'

The search for shrines and temples in Manchester threw up a lot of results and took them in some interesting directions.

One was a Roman temple in the ancient fort of Mamucium, which was the birthplace of Manchester. The fort appeared to be a very romantic setting, the sort of place where you spontaneously kiss your girl without a moment's hesitation and everything sorts itself out immediately, first in your mouth and then in your head. The temple here was a shrine of Mithras, a god who was so popular with Roman soldiers that there was actually a cult around him. Born from a rock, he hunted down bulls and attacked demons with great energy. But, clearly, he was not a goddess. The images they saw on the Internet showed him as a bearded figure, very masculine. And there was not the remotest link to coffee. Rahul wondered idly whether the ancient Romans drank coffee at all. Maybe not. He should find out.

There were several beautiful Christian churches in Manchester. But of course they would not have goddesses. St Mary's Catholic Church, built in 1794, was dedicated to a female saint, not a goddess. St George's Church at Carrington was built for Mary, the countess of Stamford. A countess, not a goddess. And, again, there was no mention of coffee at either spot.

Then there was a Hindu temple—Gita Bhavan temple—which was originally a church and now a cultural and religious centre.

Also, there was a grand cathedral. Rahul was immediately reminded of the beautiful St Thomas Cathedral near his office in Mumbai. He saw it every day on his way to Starbucks.

But across all of Manchester, they did not find a single mention of goddesses of coffee.

'Very remote possibilities, all these,' Rahul turned to Neha. 'I feel like we're missing something. I can't figure out what, but there is a missing piece. Shall we read that clue once again? And let's have some coffee as well to sharpen our brains.'

They sipped on their coffee, made using the old woman's special pink beans, which Pooviah served. Then Neha brought out the paper, stood in front of Rahul and dramatically re-read the clue.

In our own splendid Manchester lives the goddess of food.

Her shrine is a temple of coffee.

It struck her almost instantly. 'Why has the monk used the words "our own"? He was not from Manchester, so he can't call that his own city. He was from Japan.'

RG, who was around, added quite loudly, 'Japan and India, Neha. Yes, he was from Japan, but he lived a lot of his life in this part of India. He once told me, after a couple of tall tots, that he considered himself a south Indian, that even his teeth and tongue had become native to Coorg, and he went on to name some other body organs as well. What a drunken fool!'

Rahul, meanwhile, had drained his cup of coffee. His brain was suddenly feeling very light and bright, a feeling that many of us occasionally experience, and this woke him up. 'RG, you are so right. You have hit the nail on the head, actually on my dull little head. What fools we have been. "Our own splendid Manchester", that's the line. Is there a Manchester in this part of India, somewhere close by, which the monk could have called his own, because he thought of himself as a native of these parts? Some place he visited often, maybe? I am sure that is why he used those words!'

*

It took them just a few minutes of googling to discover the Manchester of south India. Sure enough, it was not too far away from the coffee plantations.

'Coimbatore, in the southernmost state of the country, is called the Manchester of south India given its extensive textile industries that are fed by the surrounding cotton fields. It houses more than twenty-five thousand small, medium and large industries, with the primary ones being textiles and engineering,' Rahul read out quickly from a website.

Another entry, by an enthusiastic blogger, was even more graphic in its description of the local Manchester:

The city has an exceptionally wonderful climate, totally unlike other towns of south India, which are generally hot and muggy. It is famous for its motor pump sets and textile mills. It is a very modern city that boasts a very ancient language. The warm people you meet here speak the historic Tamil language, which is classified as one of the great classical languages of the world. A lovely place to visit. Close by, you will find the Anaimalai wildlife sanctuary, Ooty lake, Monkey Falls and the Valparai coffee plantations.

'This must be it!' Rahul exclaimed. 'We must thank RG for his insights about the old monk, Neha. RG, where are you?'

RG was clutching his big, white mug of steaming black coffee. He had a wide smile planted on his round, white face. He was seated on a chair behind them and was examining his pocket watch with deep interest.

'Always at your service, Rahul. And yes, I do know of the monk's visit to the Valparai coffee plantations, the one that Neha and you were just talking about. He told me about it one night. He said it was one of the most rewarding visits of his life because he had found something marvellous during this short voyage.'

'What did he say? Did he talk about Coimbatore too, the Manchester of south India?'

As if on cue, RG launched into his story. 'The Valparai coffee estates are quite close to Coimbatore. Actually, you have to climb up the Anaimalai Hills from Coimbatore to reach Valparai. I have been there, when I was alive. All around is magnificent wildlife——Chinnar wildlife sanctuary, the grass hills, and the Monkey Falls. The thick forests around Valparai are teeming with animals. The lion-tailed macaque, tigers, leopards, cheetal deer, Nilgiri langurs——the coffee here is nurtured by all these wonderful animals, particularly the wild bison. You will see lots of them there, all snorting with their dangerous-looking noses and running around with sharp horns. Our monk was delighted with what he saw, and so he called Valparai the home of wildlife coffee.

'The monk stayed at Valparai for around fifteen days. He visited the places that were frequented by the famous British planter Carver Marsh, who had first planted coffee here more than a century ago. He meditated in the forests. I am told he drank copious amounts of rum with the local planters and regaled them with tales of Japan. Tall tales, I am sure. And he studied the coffees carefully. When he came back, he spoke to some of us about how the terrain was so rich in organic matter that it produced a unique washed wildlife coffee that is soft and balanced.

'But then he also spoke of his visits to Coimbatore city, on his way back from Valparai to Edobetta estate. He said one thing about Coimbatore that I will never forget. He said that he had found a shrine of coffee there, and that in that shrine was the best south Indian filter coffee he had ever tasted. Apparently, nothing else came close. I remember him calling this coffee divine nectar infused with God's own caffeine and the most wonderful aromas of Mother Earth.

'The monk was already quite old by this time. He wanted to go back to Coimbatore someday, to taste that marvellous coffee again, but he never could do that. Maybe you can follow in his footsteps now. And find his treasure too.'

'Yes, we will, RG,' Neha piped up, her excitement evident in her voice. 'And why don't you come too? You may be a ghost and all that jazz, but you are totally part of this adventure now. Let's go, let's find that shrine.'

*

Before leaving for Coimbatore, Rahul called Haroon. It had been a while since they had spoken. Haroon's booming voice was loud and clear all the way from distant Mumbai.

'So good to hear from you, Rahul! I was about to call you myself. I have some news for you, lots of good developments actually, and also a strange question about your safety. But let's talk about the good news first. Yes, yes, the Nippon Springlove mattress film is under production. Your script is great, no changes at all, nothing required as of now. And I must tell you, we have got Karthik Shah to do the film for us, the same guy who directed your famous Nidra Hair Oil film, with those two girls and all the gorgeous hair. Do you remember those long-haired chicks? I'm sure you do. Ha, ha, I know you my friend. And oh yes, Karthik will create a film which will make everyone lust and die for these blasted mattresses. He is fully tied up with his next Bollywood movie, which has the glamorous Alia Bhatt in the lead role, and you know how much I am dying to meet Alia. But for our film, he heard the script, and said, "Yes, yes, yes, I'll do it." Three times yes, to show how much he meant it. He was almost jumping on the springy mattress after I read out the script. The shoot has been fixed for exactly a month from now. I am presuming you'll be back from your holiday by then. You are the bloody scriptwriter, so we'll need your presence at the shoot of course.

'Here's another brilliant thing, Rahul. We have got actual Japanese actors to play the key characters in your film. The last shogun and two beautiful concubines. They are coming here to Mumbai in three weeks, all the way from Tokyo and Osaka. A perfect cast, all three of them. Very authentic, blue-blooded

Japanese. They will lift the film several notches. And would you believe how we arranged for them? A real stroke of luck. Take a guess, my boy.'

Rahul knew from experience that Haroon was a resourceful man, so he imagined there were many routes the man could have taken. He speculated loudly, 'One of your advertising buddies from Japan, perhaps, Haroon? Or did you visit Tokyo? I am waiting for you to tell me how you spent time with some geishas yourself, to select one for the film. Now that would be a super story, Haroon. I could write a script with that.'

'None of that, Rahul. That would be the normal way, for me. Let me tell you how. The owner of Springlove mattresses, the guy we are making this film for, came up to me a few days after he had fallen in love with your film script. Do you remember? Ram Prakash? He lives in Mysore and has now committed to us a share of his future revenues in return for this film. But let's just call him Mr Nippon for now. That's simpler.

'Mr Nippon said he had spoken to his partners from Japan, the people who are licensing him the patented mattress spring technology. They loved the film script so much that they immediately agreed to send him profiles of Japanese actors who could be the shogun and the concubines. Our director, Karthik Shah, instantly liked three of the profiles, so we selected them.

'There's something else too, Rahul. The Japanese licensor of the Springlove mattress technology will be here for the shoot. He is keen to see the whole process himself. That's quite rare, shows the total commitment that these Japanese have. That's why they won the war.'

Which war, thought Rahul. But something else stirred in his mind. 'Who's this Japanese guy, what's his name?' he asked.

Haroon took a moment to check his email and then replied, 'He is the son of the great man who discovered this mattress spring technology. Here's his name. Shinko Yamamoto. Yes, it is Yamamoto. He is the guy who sent us the details of the Japanese actors. And here's the strange question now for you.'

Rahul recognized the name immediately. Shinko Yamamoto, the brother of the bald Japanese man with the sword who appeared to be stalking them, one of the two brothers who had taken Neha and him to that strange graveyard in Tokyo.

Haroon continued, 'This Japanese guy, Yamamoto, he spoke to me on the phone. He said he was looking forward to this mattress becoming hugely popular in India. Then he said he would bring me a bottle of the finest Yamazaki eighteen-year-old whiskey when he comes to attend the film shoot in Mumbai. I accepted the offer instantly, of course. Yamazaki is lovely.

'And then he mentioned your name, Rahul. Specifically yours. He said he had narrated the story of the mattress technology to you when he met you recently at a graveyard in Tokyo. I was not sure if I heard him well, so I asked him if he really meant a graveyard, the place where dead bodies are buried? And he said, yes, a graveyard, the exact place where all the dead souls live. So, when did you go to a graveyard in Tokyo, Rahul, and why? I mean, graveyards are not your usual hangouts. A pub, or a spa, or a night club, all that I can understand. Cafés and coffee estates also given your recent obsession with coffee. But a graveyard stumps me.'

Rahul tried to briefly interrupt. 'Haroon, I can explain all this. It was a sort of dream, really.' But Haroon was in no mood to listen just then and continued speaking.

'And after saying all that, Yamamoto said something else which got me worried. He spoke in a low, grave tone. He said he knows that you will soon find a rare treasure that belongs to his family, to his brother and himself. And when you do find this treasure, you should bring it to the venue of the film shoot, a month from now, and hand it over to him. He told me this was a matter of life and death. His life and your death, that's what he said. And then, suddenly, he sounded positive. He said that there would be a rich reward for you if you were honest and handed over the treasure. I can't believe all this. Graveyards, Japanese murderers, secret treasure, rich rewards. What else is happening? Please tell me. Have you met this Yamamoto guy, Rahul? How does he know you? Are you in some sort of danger? Or is this some big practical joke all of you are playing on me? Tell me it is.'

There was silence for a minute. Haroon thought he could hear and smell Rahul sipping his coffee. And then Rahul spoke. 'It's a long story, Haroon. Difficult to explain on the phone. But don't worry, I am safe and everything's fine. Yes, there's some exciting stuff happening out here. I have to leave for Coimbatore quickly. Yes, yes, Coimbatore, the textile town in Tamil Nadu. Yes, I will take care. And I will see you at the Nippon Springlove mattress shoot in a month from now. Of course, I will tell you this entire story, every bit of it, including the graveyard in Tokyo, when we meet.'

*

While Rahul would not admit this to Haroon, there was a distinct possibility of danger from that bald, sword-bearing Japanese stalker. But any such fear was overtaken by the sheer excitement of where all this could lead Neha and him, to the monk's treasure. Who knew what it was? They had just a month to find out before the holiday ended. And then they had to decide whether to hand it over to the Yamamoto brothers who were already claiming it as their own. What was the rich reward that was being offered? What would happen if they did not find the treasure or hid it?

Questions, questions. They can come at any moment, but every answer has its time. For now, the next step led Rahul and Neha to Coimbatore, the Manchester of south India.

16

They took a train from Mysore to Coimbatore, after having driven from the coffee plantations to Mysore. The train station at Mysore, with its clock tower and colonial pillars, looked beautiful. Since they had two hours until their train arrived, they went to a museum of vintage locomotives next to the railway station. Neha could not stop looking at the old saloon on display, which had belonged to the royal family of Mysore, with its own kitchen and royal toilet, fitted like a palace on wheels.

'I could do with a carriage like that,' she told Rahul. 'I've always dreamed about long journeys on a beautiful train that goes nowhere really. It just goes on and on. Soft beds and royal toilets would fit in perfectly.'

Rahul heard her, but he was looking intently at an old sepia photograph displayed on the wall. It showed the Mysore railway station, with many people bustling all over the foreground. The photograph was grainy, but most things in it were quite visible when you went up close.

He turned to Neha and pointed to the photograph.

'Neha, do you see that?'

'See what?'

'Look at this photograph closely. Do you see those two people there in the background?'

He pointed to two figures, one of whom looked like a Buddhist monk in wide robes, carrying a small leather bag. Next to him was an Indian man with a beard and a turban on his head, carrying a luggage trunk.

'Look at that monk's face, Neha. He looks oriental. Narrow eyes, chubby face. May even be Japanese. Do you think he could be our coffee monk, the man who has set us on this chase?'

They peered closely. Yes, it could be him. Was he at this same train station several years ago, also setting out for Coimbatore and the Anaimalai Hills? And did either of these bags carry his beloved treasure?

They looked closely at the bags again. The trunk was really large. It must have had space for lots of luggage. The small leather bag, which the monk carried, looked more interesting. It had a beautifully styled handle, and a Japanese or Chinese character of some kind monogrammed on it. It appeared that they were getting their first, fuzzy glimpse of the coffee monk. But this could well be any other Chinese or Tibetan monk as well. They had heard that there were many of them in these parts, and that there was a large Tibetan monastery close by.

Just before they boarded their train to Coimbatore, they lingered at a small bookstore on the railway platform. Neha spotted a book and said excitedly, 'Hey, Rahul! Here is a book about Indian goddesses. It may just help us solve this clue.'

They bought the book and boarded the first-class compartment. As the train started moving, Neha sat back and imagined that they were the royal couple of Mysore in their own saloon with a kitchen and royal toilet. Their current compartment, while far removed from royal standards, was nicely upholstered with soft cushions. Neha dozed off, lulled by the soft motions of the train, her body leaning against Rahul's shoulders. In a few minutes, a young boy came along selling coffee in small paper cups. Neha woke up to a nice cup of strong, milky, sugary coffee.

Then, they began reading the book on Indian goddesses. Would it help them find the answer to the second cryptic clue:

In our own splendid Manchester lives the goddess of food.
Her shrine is a temple of coffee.

The book had so many stories that they got completely absorbed in it for a couple of hours, fascinated by things they had never known before. Neha began reading a few stories aloud and Rahul listened silently with keen interest.

'Goddesses in the Hindu religion protect the good and destroy the evil. They embody Shakti, or power, to do both these acts. Along with the male gods, they complete the divinity of the universe beautifully and powerfully. Durga is the warrior goddess who combats all the evil forces that threaten the good. She is worshipped during Durga Puja, the festival of Navaratri. Ferocious and powerful, she is often shown demolishing Mahishasur, the evil demon god, with the help of her sharp weapons which she holds in her multiple hands. She represents feminine power, and the tiger is her vehicle. She is also known by other names like Adi Parashakti, Amba and Bhavani. Lakshmi is the goddess of wealth, prosperity, fortune and fertility. She is worshipped during Diwali, the annual festival of lights where Indians prepare to welcome the goddess into their homes. Lakshmi is the wife of Vishnu, one of the three primary gods of the Hindu pantheon. She holds a lotus in her hand, a symbol of fortune. Her vehicle, quite curiously, is the owl, though sometimes it is also a white elephant.'

Neha paused here. 'Very interesting, Rahul. But I don't think our clue refers to either Durga or Lakshmi. We need the goddess of food. To tell you the truth though, I love Durga. She shows us the power that women possess within themselves all the time. I wish I were like Durga.'

Rahul nodded. 'Yes, Neha. You know, we will need our own Durga if that Japanese guy turns up again with his sword. It worries me that either his brother or he has already telephoned Haroon threatening and asking for the treasure to be handed over. Well, we haven't found it yet, and how are we even sure that we will find it? But read your book, read on. Let's check out the other goddesses.'

'Saraswati is the goddess of wisdom, knowledge, music and the arts. She is worshipped during the festival of Basant Panchami, also known as Saraswati Puja. Young children are taught to write the alphabet on this day, a sort of christening of their long voyage into the world of knowledge. Saraswati is depicted with the veena in her hands. She has the powers of healing and purifying, and she rides the swan. Parvati is the goddess of fertility, love and devotion. She is the gentle form of Durga and she nurtures humanity. She is often regarded as the Mother Goddess in the Hindu religion. Along with Lakshmi and Saraswati, she forms the trinity of goddesses who are worshipped by Hindus. Parvati is the wife of Shiva, the central deity of many famous temples in India. She provides the god his recreative energy.'

'It's neither Saraswati nor Parvati,' said Neha with some regret in her voice. As she scanned the next page, she held her breath and said almost triumphantly, 'Rahul, I think we've got her now. Here's the goddess we are looking for. Here she is.'

Neha continued reading, now with excitement, 'Annapoorna is the goddess of food and nourishment. She is a very popular deity and is shown as a youthful goddess with a reddish complexion, round face and four hands. In one hand, she holds a vessel full of delicious food. In another, she has a golden ladle with which she can give out food to her devotees. She is believed to be an avatar, or form, of Parvati. Her name, Annapoorna, is composed of the Sanskrit words "annam", which means food; and "poorna", which means filled with. She is said to have one thousand names.'

Rahul took the book away from Neha's hands and read the section quickly. 'Yes, Neha, that's so cool and feels so correct. She is the goddess of food, all right. So, we have to look for a shrine, a temple of Goddess Annapoorna in the town of Coimbatore. That should not be very challenging. I suggest we walk into the first temple we see and ask the local priest there. He should know.'

For the rest of the journey, they spoke about many other things. It was mostly Neha speaking because she felt strangely relaxed and reassured today, sitting close to Rahul in a train. Something about him was growing nicely in her mind, like a tiny little coffee bush.

'I love blogging about food and drinks, Rahul. If you've read all my blogs, you know that's who I am. I think that's why I have come to like coffee so much. Coffee is a wonderful thing for a blogger like me; it makes for so many interesting stories. And of course, it helps that you too love coffee. I want to experience coffee and write about it like no one has before. Who knows, maybe I can get the world to discover totally new things about Indian coffee!

'Now, listen to me. Here's a beautiful story about a very special coffee that I discovered in a book when we were staying at that bungalow in the coffee plantations. It's a story about the tribe of Araku Valley in south India and the brilliant coffee that they grow. This valley is home to one hundred and fifty different tribal communities and is located in the Eastern Ghats, very close to Vishakapatnam and Odisha. This tribe grows one of the finest organic coffees on the face of the earth. Did you know that, Rahul, you avid lover of coffee? I bet you did not.'

She poked him playfully and continued.

'The coffee grown in Araku Valley has a fruity and caramel flavour, which is unique when it comes to coffee, Rahul. It is incredibly smooth and leaves a lovely, silky aftertaste in your mouth. That's what I have read. Fruity and caramel coffee with a silky flavour. Wow! That's simply magic. And here's the thing about this special tribal coffee. The people who grow it are Adivasis who take care of their coffee like their own children.

They nurture it throughout the year. Each tribal farmer has his own little coffee farm. All this love is paid off in creating a real masterpiece, Rahul. Just last year, Araku coffee won the gold medal at the Prix Epicures in Paris, beating the best varieties of coffee from places like Sumatra and Colombia. Isn't that marvellous? Why don't we go someplace that serves us Araku Valley coffee? We could have a long, lingering cup together.'

Rahul was enjoying hearing Neha speak. Her words tumbled into each other nicely. He kept looking at her wide eyes, which spoke their own language. He knew that both of them had liked each other ever since they had first met at a party in Mumbai a couple of years ago. He loved reading her blog, which was becoming increasingly popular on social media. But here he was now, seeing her passion for coffee and for storytelling, flowing so free like a pure and sparkling river.

He moved closer, put his arms around her and held her in a soft embrace. He thought to himself, *yes, we could have a long, lingering cup together, Neha. Maybe every morning, freshly brewed, in our own home.*

*

They walked down the wide roads of Coimbatore like a young couple in love. Rahul Kamath in his khaki shorts and green shirt, with a cap on his head, and Neha Sharma in her denim-blue jeans, with a close cropped yellow top. It was very hot and they were licking their ice cream waffle cones as they ambled along on Race Course Road. No one looking at them could ever imagine that they were here in the search of a monk's treasure, or were being stalked by a strange, bald Japanese man.

Strangely, they missed RG's presence. He was not with them because he could only travel within the coffee plantations in Coorg, or close by. Ghosts have strict boundaries in the afterlife, which is why ghosts who haunt one place are generally not found in other places. RG had bid them goodbye as they left Cottabetta Bungalow and wished them well in their search.

'We will meet again for sure,' he had said as Rahul and Neha left the coffee plantations. Holding his coffee mug, he went on, 'I have enjoyed my coffee time with you. Ghosts like me are so lonely all the time, you know. I am so happy that you are searching for the monk's long-hidden secret treasure. It deserves to be found by people who really love coffee with all their heart. I think you are destined to find it, that's why you were sent here in the first place, and that's why the monk has guided you so far. I will rest forever once the treasure is found, Rahul and Neha. Enjoy Coimbatore; it's a nice and easy place. I will see you when you are back. I think you will be back soon.'

Meanwhile, as soon as Rahul and Neha saw a temple by the street, they walked in. It was a small shrine built for Lord Vinayaka, the elephant-headed god. The walls were painted red and white in alternate strips. Inside, a single priest, bare-chested and dressed in his traditional white dhoti, was preparing the idol for some rituals.

Rahul asked him, 'Sir, do you know where we can find a temple of Goddess Annapoorna?'

The priest looked at them for a while before answering, 'Why do you want to know?'

'Sir, we have been asked to go there. My wife and I, we were told by our family astrologer to pray there. This is for a blessing we have been seeking for a long time. Today, under the right confluence of stars, we want to find this temple. We have come all the way from Mumbai.' He held Neha's hand to indicate that it was a joint blessing they were seeking.

This time, she did not kick Rahul. Instead, she silently admired the way Rahul was spinning his story.

The priest turned out to be cooperative. 'In that case, it is important you go there right away, before the stars disperse. You two have come to the right place. The famous temple of Goddess Annapoorna is not too far from here. Hire a rickshaw to go to R.S. Puram and ask for Annapoorneswari Temple. It is a big and famous shrine dedicated to the goddess. It is more than five hundred years old.'

Rahul and Neha arrived at the ancient temple to find it teeming with people. The entrance tower, called the gopuram, was ornate in its design and an impressive piece of architecture. Rahul could see small sculptures of various goddesses embedded at various points in the gopuram. Exquisite carvings adorned it. He stood staring at the temple for some time, taken by its timeless beauty.

Within the temple, they saw the silver idol of Shiva begging Annapoorneswari for food with a skull pot in his hand. This was a depiction of a famous Hindu legend in which Shiva asks for food from the goddess to relieve him of a curse. Only food from the goddess's hands could purify him again.

They walked around a little bit, seeing the pilgrims pray and looking at trees which were interestingly named after the planets.

However, nowhere could they see a shrine of coffee or anything that even reminded them of it:

In our own splendid Manchester lives the goddess of food.
Her shrine is a temple of coffee.

A priest who was watching them came up and spoke. He wore a pigtail and a large holy mark on his forehead.

'Would you like to offer special prayers? People come here to pray for food, health and also marriage negotiations.'

Neha looked up at Rahul. Marriage negotiations. What an interesting and archaic thought! She said nothing. Instead, she asked the priest, 'Is there a shrine of coffee in this temple? Can you show us the way?'

The priest looked at her with an incredulous expression.

'Coffee? Madam, you are inside a sacred temple. We don't have shrines of coffee here; we have shrines of our gods and goddesses. I think you have come to the wrong place if you are looking for coffee. But maybe I can offer a special prayer for your health?'

Neha, however, wasn't one to give up so easily. 'Are you sure? Is there a coffee plant anywhere here, like these trees that are named after planets? Annapoorneswari is the goddess of food, and coffee is food too, isn't it?'

The priest, too, was stubborn. In fact, he appeared to be relishing the opportunity to make his points about the temple, which had been his home for over twenty years now. He spoke in fluent English, his pigtail moving from side to side as he answered.

'Madam, don't take me lightly. This is a holy place. Food for our goddess is that which nourishes people. She offers nourishment and health. She provides rice, grains, pulses and vegetables. Coffee is not considered food in our temple. Far from it. I have never heard of a shrine of coffee, Madam. You will not find one here, or in any other temple. Now, I have to go. There are many pilgrims here who need me.'

Rahul and Neha looked at each other. They had got so far in their search for the treasure, but now they were stuck again. They were right here, in the temple of the goddess of food, in the Manchester of south India, but without an answer to the second clue and no idea about what to do next. Had they reached a dead end?

'Let's have a nice cup of hot coffee, Neha,' said Rahul. 'Often, it's the coffee which has all the answers. Also, I am feeling tired, as are you. It's been a long day.'

Just as they stepped out through the gopuram, they saw him once again. Takahira Yamamoto. This time, he was accompanied by another man who looked Japanese too but was somewhat taller and had a very thin face. Yamamoto looked at Rahul and Neha. Their eyes locked. They were just a couple of feet away from each other. Contact seemed unavoidable this time. Rahul offered a silent prayer and hoped that there would be no violence.

Takahira Yamamoto drew out his sword and held it high in the air. He looked at Rahul and Neha, and spoke in staccato English.

'The treasure,' he said, 'my family's treasure. Don't forget, it is mine. I see every move you make, Rahul and Neha. Everywhere you go. I watch you from far and I watch you from near. But I watch you. Do you remember Yanaka-reien in Tokyo, where I took you? A graveyard is a sad place of memories, a terrible place of death. You do not want to be carried to the graveyard, my young friends. You have many years of life before you. Don't try to take away what belongs to my family.'

Rahul stood silent, his left hand shielding Neha lest the crazy Japanese man bring down his sword. And while the man may be crazy, the sword looked real. Its polished steel was gleaming under the hot Coimbatore sun. By now, a few bystanders and pilgrims had gathered around them. It was not every day that a foreigner bearing a sword appeared in front of Annapoorneswari Temple. The priest they had spoken to earlier had left the pilgrims he was assisting and turned up too.

Takahira Yamamoto was not in the least concerned with the motley crowd. In an emphatic movement, he lowered his sword and the people moved back immediately. He put the sword back into its leather scabbard, which was attached loosely to the belt of his trousers. He glared at Rahul and stared at him for a full minute. Then he walked away with the tall, thin man who had remained completely silent all this while. Both the men boarded an orange car that was waiting, the same Tata Nexon that Rahul had seen during their earlier encounter in Suntikoppa.

After Takahira was gone, Neha turned to Rahul, 'I need that coffee now, Rahul, to calm my nerves. Also, we need to talk. Seriously. Why are we crossing swords with this weird Japanese man? Just why, why are we searching for this treasure that we know absolutely nothing about? Tell me that.'

Rahul felt the same. He was tired too. Maybe they should call off this search right there and return to Mumbai, safe, alive and far away from Japanese cemeteries. For him, it would be back to writing advertising scripts. For Neha, it would be back to blogging about food. In any case, their search had reached a dead end since there was no coffee shrine in the temple of Goddess Annapoorna. This was the end of their little adventure. *It was good as long as it lasted*, he thought.

He turned to an elderly man standing near them, wearing a white dhoti and blue shirt.

'Sir, where can we find the best coffee here? My wife and I are visiting from Mumbai and we need a cup of coffee.'

Again, Neha did not kick Rahul when she heard the word 'wife'. Instead, she stood there looking nervous and tired.

The elderly man didn't even blink before responding. The passion in his voice totally exceeded the response that such a simple question would normally evoke. Usually, a person would simply point to a place and offer directions to a neighbouring coffee shop. This man, however, said, 'Young man, you are very lucky. Just ten minutes away, on the nearby road, you will find the best coffee on earth. Just ask for Sree Annapoorna Hotel. Everyone here knows it so you will not have a problem finding it. It is not just a hotel; it is our city's most famous temple of coffee.'

Rahul's eyes nearly popped out. Sree Annapoorna Hotel, the temple of coffee, the same name as the goddess of food. This was staggering. This was beautiful. Actually, this was unbelievable.

'Thank you, Sir. Yes, we are lucky. Actually, Sir, you have brought us luck. We will go there. Come on, Neha! Let's walk down to this place quickly and taste the best coffee in the world.'

As they walked, Rahul felt the zing popping back into his mind and waves of energy bouncing back into his body.

'Listen, Neha. I know you think we should give up. Yes, that Japanese guy is crazy and weird. Totally. I buy that. But did you see what just happened? Did you hear what the old man said? Just when we thought we were stuck, he helped us with the second clue. This is a sign, Neha, a divine signal that we are destined to find this treasure. Maybe, it is a sign from the old monk. It very well could be a signal from the goddess herself.'

The words tumbled out of Rahul's mouth. Neha looked at him. When he spoke like that, Rahul was not just charming to her, he was irresistible. Like a man on a mission. That was how she had seen him when they first spoke at the party in Mumbai, two years ago. 'I have to write the best advertising films on earth, Neha, I simply have to, because that's what I've been born for. Let me tell you how I write my scripts, late at night on my balcony with a glass of red wine . . .' She remembered that conversation very well because it had very nearly seduced her. She looked at him once again and smiled.

'Yes, I hear you, Rahul. But we need to talk. Let's chat over coffee.'

17

The temple of coffee that Rahul and Neha were seeking was located at one end of a busy road that cut through the heart of Coimbatore, housing merchants who dealt in textiles, jewellery and earthenware. You could see merchants waiting expectantly for business, all of them dressed in traditional white dhotis and starched white shirts, sporting big ash-grey tilaks on their foreheads. Interestingly, on this road there were a number of pawnbrokers who offered loans against jewellery or other valuable items as collateral.

In the olden days, a large burial ground was situated adjacent to this road with stories of ghosts and ghouls enjoying a free rein here. But parts of that burial ground had later been converted into a playground, as a result of which all this talk had died down completely. Had Neha known of this history, she may have been at risk of a nervous breakdown. At that point, she wanted to be as far away as possible from ghosts, graveyards and burial grounds.

They asked a passing local for the way to the hotel and he readily pointed it out to them. They turned around a corner and saw the large sign ahead of them on an imposing building: Sree

Annapoorna Hotel. They walked in and immediately sensed the delicious aroma of coffee. It was a moist fragrance, brimming with the warm, heady flavours of coffee and milk. Rahul saw Neha stop, take in a deep breath and close her eyes in happiness. He thought to himself, when there are such wonderful flavours in the air, all of us should pause and take a deep breath. These aromas are too valuable to waste.

They asked a bearer for two cups of coffee. 'Can I get you our special filter coffee?' the bearer asked. Rahul and Neha nodded.

The coffee came quickly, served in small brass tumblers with a layer of froth on top. Rahul took a small sip and felt complete bliss. He had never tasted something as delicious as this. He saw Neha too sit up in delight after taking a few sips.

'Rahul, what wonderful coffee is this? We have never had something like this before. These flavours are playing so beautifully with my tongue and this is such a brilliant melange of coffee notes. Oh my God! I can write a thousand blogs about this coffee, Rahul.'

Her fatigue seemed to have disappeared by now. All she wanted to speak about was the coffee. She began waving both her arms animatedly as she spoke. 'Fabulous coffee, Rahul. Just heavenly.'

A senior bearer, or maybe he was the manager of the hotel since he appeared to be authoritative, saw her delight and came up to their table. 'Madam, I can see you like our filter coffee. Let me tell you about it. This coffee is made of the finest blend of beans, roasted to perfection. We have a secret recipe that makes this filter coffee the best. Oh yes, it is the best, and only very fresh milk is used. See its golden colour.'

She looked at her cup for a moment, admiring the colour, and then continued listening to the man. 'People come here every day for coffee, Madam. This is not just coffee. It is our way of life. Coffee like this is a luxury that everyone can enjoy. Welcome to Annapoorna Coffee, Madam,' he said.

Rahul and Neha sat there quietly, savouring their moment of glorious Coimbatore coffee. They silently agreed with the elderly man who had guided them there, telling them that this was the best coffee on earth. It had certainly heightened their senses. All their exhaustion was now behind them.

After some time, Rahul looked up from his tumbler and said, 'Do you remember what RG told us, Neha? That the monk had come to a place in Coimbatore where he had found the best coffee on earth? I think he actually said that it was divine nectar infused with caffeine. I am sure this is the place, Neha. It is named after the goddess of food, Annapoorna, and it is certainly a shrine of coffee. With such heavenly coffee, can there be a higher shrine at all? I think this place is certainly the answer to the second clue. Let's figure it out now. How about two more cups of this wonderful coffee to stimulate our minds?'

They had some more coffee and then there was one more surprise waiting for them. The elderly man in the white dhoti and blue shirt who had initially guided them to this hotel appeared in front of them.

'You had dropped this envelope and paper in front of the temple. It probably fell out of your pocket when you were speaking to that Japanese man,' he told Rahul, handing him an envelope and a folded sheet of paper. 'I knew where you were headed, so I came here quickly.'

Rahul recognized it immediately. It was the monk's paper with the second clue written on it.

In our own splendid Manchester lives the goddess of food.
Her shrine is a temple of coffee.

'Thank you, Sir. Yes, this is mine. It was careless of me to have dropped it. Thank you so much for bringing it back to me.'

As he took the paper, he saw something else written on the back of the paper, in a similar ink. Just four words, but in the same writing style:

Ask pawnbroker Ramaswamy.

Rahul had missed the reverse side of the note earlier, but these words were clearly legible now. Here was the monk, telling them what to do next. Before he could tell Neha about what they had missed, the man took a look at their empty cups and began speaking. 'How did you like the filter coffee here?'

Rahul was genuinely thankful to him and so he replied, 'This is surely the best coffee in the world. Why don't you join us for a cup? My wife and I will be delighted.'

Again, there was no kick from under the table. The man took them up on the offer immediately. He seemed happy for the company. Over the next hour, he spoke to them about the simple joys of filter coffee, a beautiful rambling conversation they would not forget for a long time.

*

The elderly man sipped his coffee from the tumbler and spoke with deep conviction about a very wide range of matters related to coffee, additionally emphasizing every sentence to underline his knowledge and authority.

'Is coffee just another product? No, Sir. Is coffee just a thirst quencher? No, Sir. Is coffee merely an experience in a restaurant? Again, no, Sir. I tell you, Sir, coffee is religion, nothing less. It is sacred, it has beautiful rituals, it cleanses our minds and it makes our hearts dance.

'Beautiful rituals of selecting the beans, making the blend, roasting the coffee, powdering it fresh for the day's filter coffee, rituals of visiting the neighbouring coffee works, small shops that grind this powder for us, with love and care. These shops know their coffee very well, as they roast and grind it to such perfect colour and shape. And then, finally, the aroma diffuses in your kitchen at the break of dawn, as the coffee drips into the filter. I tell you, coffee is as glorious as the rising sun.

'What we are drinking now is the finest filter coffee. But all filter coffee is not the same, Sir. Don't ever make that common mistake. This is Coimbatore-style filter coffee, although every city around here that is worth its weight in coffee beans has its own style of making coffee. Oh yes, you will find Madras filter kaapi, Mysore filter coffee and even Kumbakonam degree coffee.

Rahul and Neha were struck by the reference to degree coffee. 'What is degree coffee?' asked Neha.

'What is degree coffee, you want to know? Madam, I will tell you. It is very high-quality coffee. Fresh milk of the highest degree of purity is used in the very first decoction of the brew that gives the best flavour. I tell you, this is like coffee that has earned its PhD degree.'

Then Rahul asked the man a question about chicory and coffee. Something he had always wanted to know. The old man responded with renewed passion.

'Ah, Sir, you want to know about chicory. Let me tell you, it's just a root. Some people here love their filter coffee blended with chicory. Not me, sir. Chicory will never, ever enter my house. I have told my wife and my children that adding chicory is like adulterating your coffee. No adulteration for me. I like my coffee pure, nothing but the best beans, milk and sugar. That's the way God wants us to have our coffee.

'Coffee elevates music. Listen to pure classical music over a hot cup of coffee. I tell you, Sir, the experience is magical. I have done it several times, so I can tell you from experience, the music has revealed itself to me through coffee in very special ways.

'Why does this hotel serve the world's best coffee? It's because of their unique blend and secret roasting recipe. The founder made this recipe over fifty years ago. It has not changed since then. It has been passed on from father to son. The owner will never reveal it to anyone. People from all over the world—Americans, Germans, Japanese and so on—they come here and they all agree. You have to taste this coffee at least once to make your life worthwhile. Like a pilgrimage, Sir. A coffee pilgrimage.'

At the end of an hour, the elderly man thanked Rahul and Neha for the coffee and left as silently as he had arrived. Rahul and Neha were amazed at everything they had heard. They felt refreshed.

Rahul then showed Neha the four words written on the back of the paper:

Ask pawnbroker Ramaswamy

Neha found herself strangely excited once again. She was piped up, fortified by the world's best filter coffee now sloshing in her guts.

'Rahul, forget what I said earlier about not going ahead. This adventure is taking us into some really interesting areas. What a wonderful sermon about coffee this was. That man should be writing a million blogs. All the coffee lovers will make him rich. Now, suddenly, we have our next clue. This is our own adventure, yours and mine, Rahul. To tell you the truth, I am a little worried about the Japanese weirdo, but I can live with that noise and drama for some more time because this is really getting exciting.'

This was exactly what Rahul wanted to hear. He leant over, kissed her and then held her hand.

'Yes, Neha. We will deal with the bald Japanese man when we have to. Let him stalk us for all I care. He hasn't done anything yet, apart from waving his ridiculous-looking sword. This is the most glorious coffee adventure ever and we happen to be right in the middle of it. The way our coffee monk has laid out his clues, I am sure there is a lot more about coffee that we have to discover. We'll definitely remember this all our lives.'

'Yes, Rahul. I agree. And then there's the final secret too. Come on, let's find pawnbroker Ramaswamy. He must be somewhere close to this place because he is part of the same clue.'

18

As Rahul and Neha left Sree Annapoorna Hotel with its fabled filter coffee behind them, they saw a long line of pawnbrokers' stores on the main road adjacent to the hotel. These stores were visible from the windows of the hotel and they silently thanked the monk for placing his clues so well. He was a smart monk for sure.

A range of interesting names and descriptions met their eyes. Golden Pawnbrokers, Gold and Silver Loans; Shobana Pawn Shop, Loan against Gold; Balaji Pawnbrokers, Second-hand Gold Coin Buyers; Dream Loan Pawn Company, Loans for all Your Dreams; Pandyan Gold, Bring Your Gold to us Today.

Pawnbrokers were an important part of the community here. People who wanted loans would come here, offer their jewellery as collateral and be granted a loan immediately at a specified interest rate. They would get back their jewellery when they had paid the loan in full, along with the accumulated interest. If they did not repay the loan in time, the pawn broker could sell off the jewellery to other people. Of course, jewellery was not the only currency these shops accepted—electronics, firearms and even musical instruments served as currency.

Most of the shops looked old and dusty. Rahul chose to walk into Dream Loan Pawn Company first. A young man, presumably an assistant, was glued to his mobile phone. He looked at them grumpily, not too happy at the interruption.

'Owner has gone out for lunch, Sir. Please come back later. After 4 p.m.'

'We are not here to meet your owner, boy. We want to ask you a simple question. We are searching for someone.'

'All right, ask your question. Not sure that I will know the answer. But I've been here for long enough to know most people. Also, I won't help you for free since my master hardly pays me well. How can a person live on a pittance in this costly city?'

'We will pay you well if you answer me. Do you know of a person called pawnbroker Ramaswamy?'

'Who does not know him, Sir? He is the oldest pawnbroker in this area. Must be more than two hundred years old, or even more than that. Everyone knows him, but all of us avoid him. Who wants to listen to his long and boring stories?'

'Good, good. Where is Ramaswamy's shop? Where can we meet him?'

'Give me my money, Sir. Then I will tell you.'

They gave him a Rs 100 note and the young boy promptly said, 'Around twenty shops away from here, Sir, on the left side of the road. The board says Ramaswamy Pawn Shop. It is quite easy to find. Ramaswamy Ayya has put his own name on the shop.'

Rahul chided himself. They could have saved the money had they walked a little further. But he smiled and thanked the boy.

Ramaswamy Pawn Shop was a small and dingy den. An old wooden door opened into a tiny room with a small reclining wooden desk placed on a raised platform. There was a cupboard with glass doors, mostly displaying silver trophies that must have been pawned here. At one end of the room stood a steel almirah. A bulky ceiling fan, very old and covered with dust, was rotating slowly right on top. Behind the wooden desk, writing something in a thick, bound notebook, sat an old man wearing thick spectacles. His face was wrinkled but his eyes appeared very sharp.

After a few minutes, he looked up at them and asked, 'What do you want? I have never seen you before.'

Neha picked up the conversation. 'Are you Mr Ramaswamy?'

'Didn't you see the name of my shop? Yes, I am Ramaswamy. Who else can I be? And who are you two?'

'We have been sent here by a Japanese monk, Sir. My name is Neha. This is my husband, Rahul. We have come all the way from Mumbai. I think we have some long-pending business with you.'

Rahul smiled. He did not kick her either.

Ramaswamy peered at them intently for a few minutes. He then looked them up and down, frowning. 'What is the name of this monk, where is he from?'

'Saito is his name. He is a monk from the coffee estates of Coorg.'

When Ramaswamy heard the answer, his face lost its frown and broke out into a broad smile. 'I have been waiting so many

139

years now for you to come here. Welcome to my little pawn store. Sit down, sit down. Let me get your parcel. It has been gathering dust in my almirah for so long.'

Ramaswamy stood up, surprisingly sprightly for his age, and walked to the steel almirah. He unlocked it with a big metal key and brought out a brown parcel from one of the lower shelves. It was wrapped in paper and tied with thick, strong string. He set this in front of Rahul and Neha and said, 'That monk, Saito, he spent five days with me around thirty years ago. He told me many stories about faraway lands and various types of coffees. Drank lots of coffee, mostly at Annapoorna Hotel nearby. Gave me a gold coin too, with some markings on it. Very knowledgeable person. I enjoyed his company and learnt a lot about coffee. Then, he left this parcel with me. He asked me to keep it safe and hand it over to someone who would come here, but only if they mentioned his name correctly. And, he added, that if I retired before these people came, I was to hand it over to my son for safekeeping.

'But here you are and here I am, still hale and hearty. Ninety-five years old and still going strong. You know why? It is because I drink the best coffee in the world every day from Annapoorna. Good coffee is the secret behind a long life. And listen to me, I know nothing of what is inside this parcel, so be careful when you open it. I am just doing my duty for that monk. I have been carrying this weight all these years and I am happy that you have come to collect it. The monk was a good man. I wonder where he is now.'

Rahul replied, 'Sir, he passed away many years ago on his coffee plantation.'

Then he added an improvization, 'You will be happy to know, Sir, that he died peacefully and happily, surrounded by more than a hundred types of his favourite coffee beans. His servant tells us that all those coffee beans rolled over in tribute to him as soon as he breathed his last. Lived with coffee and died with coffee, Sir. Now, we are just following his instructions.'

Ramaswamy looked at them again. 'A peaceful death is a good farewell. May his soul rest in peace. I hope you find what you are looking for inside this packet. Would you like to stay and talk? I have a very interesting story to tell you about what happened to our pawnbroking business during the Second World War.'

PART C

THE FINAL CLUE

19

Neha was in a tearing hurry to open the parcel, to see where the monk would lead them next. She ripped open the brown paper, twisted the twine off the packet and found a tin inside, its lid held down firmly with tape.

It was one of those old square tins that were used to pack sweets or biscuits. Neha could read the faint words 'Parry's Lacto Bon Bons' on it. She remembered the brown, plastic-wrapped sweets from her childhood. Lacto Bon Bons. The tin itself featured characters from fairy tales like the ugly duckling, the tin soldier, the little mermaid, a blue nightingale and an emperor marching without his clothes, all painted in an attractive melange of blue, orange and white. The tin in front of her now was an old chocolate tin designed to appeal to young children but made of sturdy metal that had remained intact all these years. *What exciting message would this tin contain?* She pulled the tape away, opened the lid and turned to Rahul.

She then pulled out a cloth pouch of coffee similar to the ones that had accompanied the first two clues. The same, familiar walnutty smell of the old woman's magical coffee beans assailed their nostrils. Rahul smelt it deeply and thought to himself, *this is the defining smell of our adventure.* For a moment, his mind drifted a little. *Why this adventure alone, every milestone in life has a smell associated with it.* He should do something unique and memorable with smells when writing scripts in the future. He tucked away this thought for now and returned the pouch to Neha.

Then they found an envelope folded at the bottom of the tin. It had the monk's familiar scrawly handwriting.

> The second shrine of coffee you have now left behind. The filter coffee here is the best man can find. Now to the third shrine you head, and then you are near. Open my little puzzle and go without fear.

It was clear that this merry monk liked nice and simple rhymes. They opened the envelope. There was a paper inside with two simple lines written on it. This was the third clue.

> Goddess from the sea, you welcome our coffee.
> Rain and mellow, we are gold and yellow.

Rahul looked at Neha and smiled. This was as cryptic as ever. They had no clue about what it meant, but wouldn't it be great fun to solve this and inch closer to the secret treasure that the monk had left behind?

Neha said, 'Rahul, turn the page over. Let's see whether there is anything written on the other side. You know, like the "go ask pawnbroker Ramaswamy" note that we saw quite late last time around.'

They turned the page and there it was, one more line in the same handwriting:

Every coffee bean tells a story, including my own, says the goddess.

Goddess from the sea? A goddess who owns coffee beans? What was the monk trying to tell them? Who *was* this third goddess?

They had found the first two goddesses after a considerable search, thanks to some timely help from RG and a little bit of luck. Unfortunately, RG was not around now. And luck, by its very nature, cannot be relied on all the time.

First, they had discovered the shrine of Goddess Kaveri, at whose birthplace they had found the remarkable bellada kaapi, the lovely coffee made with jaggery. That had led them to Goddess Annapoorna, the goddess of food, whose name had inspired the finest filter coffee they had ever tasted. Where, now, would this take them?

Neha had an idea.

'Rahul, let's go back to that book we picked up at the Mysore station, the one about Indian goddesses. That should give us all the possible details on this subject. I even saw a large glossary at the end, with names of more than four hundred goddesses. We need the name of the goddess from the sea. That should be easy enough—we Hindus have gods and goddesses for just about everything.'

And so, in their hotel room that night, overlooking the Coimbatore race course, Rahul and Neha pored over the book. They read every chapter on every goddess: Ganga, Yamuna, Saraswati, Mumbadevi, Kamakhya, Bhagya, Parvati, Durga, Kali, and many more. They learnt the legends associated with these goddesses, about the temples built to honour them, what each goddess stood for, the animals or birds that were their *vahanas* (vehicles) and the prayers offered at their shrines. They found everything possible, except a goddess from the sea. The book was conspicuously silent on that specific subject.

*

'Call me. Need to brief you quickly about the Nippon film shoot,' said the text message from Haroon.

When Rahul called, Haroon was in an expansive mood.

'We are three weeks away from the shoot, Rahul. Everything's set. Your holiday should be done by then. This is going to be one of the most iconic ad films of the year; I can feel it, that's why I'm so excited. No Indian brand has ever done a film with an authentic shogun. Your script was so fantastic, Rahul, what a masterstroke! That's what excited Mr Nippon and his Japanese principals in the first place, you know. The film makes its point so beautifully and precisely. Who knows, we may even win an award at Cannes.'

Haroon was daydreaming now. Rahul knew this film was good and he was also sure it would do a lot to boost the sales of Nippon Springlove mattresses. But he didn't believe for a moment that it was the kind of film that would be recognized at the Cannes festival. However, he kept quiet because Haroon continued speaking.

'And there's some more good news too. The two Japanese girls who are playing the concubines in this film will be here a week before the date. They want to see India and get used to our climatic conditions generally, you know what I mean. I've seen their photographs and, let me tell you, I spoke to one of them yesterday. A very friendly girl who is totally keen to explore India. We may just want to take them out to dinner and a couple of nice evenings out. We don't meet Japanese babes that often in Mumbai, if you know what I mean. We could do Wasabi at Taj, treat them to a nice Japanese meal, Rahul. Or if they show an interest in eating Indian seafood, maybe the Konkan Café or Trishna.'

Rahul didn't fancy spending long evenings with Haroon and two Japanese girls he had never met. Haroon was a good boss, but when he got drunk, well, it was best to avoid him. Previous evenings of this kind had never gone well. But before he could respond, Haroon continued his monologue.

'By the way, Rahul, that Japanese principal guy, Yamamoto, he's called me a couple of times. He says that his brother saw you in some small town, heading to a pawnbroker's store. He says they are tracking you very carefully; he desperately wants to get hold of some treasure that belongs to his family. I am amazed; I am totally lost, Rahul. I mean, what were you doing at a pawnbroker's place? The last time it was a cemetery, now it is a pawnbroker. Are you on holiday or some sort of crazy suicide mission? I thought you were on a coffee trail in the plantations. How do graveyards and pawnbrokers figure there?'

Rahul didn't see the point of this conversation. 'I will tell you all about this when I am back, Haroon. Yes, I am in the middle of some exciting stuff here, but it is too much trouble to explain over the phone.'

'That's fine. I don't need all the lurid details now. I'm just worried about what will happen if you come here without that treasure that Yamamoto wants. I have a neat solution for that too, Rahul, if you need it. Even if you don't actually find any treasure, and I doubt you will find anything at all, just buy something valuable that looks like real Japanese treasure. We can say that's what you found and give it to that guy who's making these strange phone calls to me. I am sure we can find something fairly authentic at a couple of antique stores here in Mumbai. I'll pay for it officially too, these are our clients and they are paying us well. So, don't worry about the cost as long as it is reasonable.'

And then he turned his focus back on to the Nippon film. 'Three weeks, Rahul. That's the countdown to the best film we have ever made. Nippon Springlove. Your film, and mine too. Don't get into any more trouble, my friend. Be safe. And actually, you know what, focus on coffee. Just focus on coffee. You love coffee, that's the real purpose of your holiday, not some ridiculous Japanese treasure that has nothing to do with us. That's how you will find the right things to do and also stay safe. Sayonara.' The Japanese sign-off was a nice Haroon-ish touch.

After Haroon put the phone down, Rahul sat back and looked at Neha, who was still asleep, curled up softly on the bed in their room. Haroon's words kept coming back to his mind. 'Just focus on coffee . . . That's how you will find the right things to do.'

Whatever Haroon may have meant by these words, they had struck a chord.

Yes, Rahul told himself, Neha and he had, so far, found the right things to do by focusing on coffee. It was the story of the river goddess who nurtured coffee in Coorg that had led them to solving the first clue. It was coffee that had helped them crack the second clue. On the first reading, the monk's clues may revolve around goddesses and rivers and food, but it was suddenly clear to him that their essence lay in coffee. That was the beverage the monk loved and lived with, the one that Rahul loved too. Haroon was right, they should focus on coffee once again to solve this new clue, and not just on some Hindu goddess of the sea, who may not exist at all. *Thanks, Haroon! That was extraordinary insight, coming from you. Here's hoping you have a great time with those Japanese babes!*

He looked at the line once again and kept staring at it for some time.

Goddess from the sea, you welcome our coffee.
Rain and mellow, we are gold and yellow.

When Neha woke up, Rahul was ready with a plan. 'Hey, Neha, I think I know what we should do. Let's dump the goddess in the sea for now and look for coffee that has something to do with the rain, and probably has a mellow taste. I think that will lead us to a good place.'

20

They were back in the Cottabetta Bungalow the next day. Pooviah welcomed them with great warmth.

'Sir, Madam, welcome, welcome. Your room is ready. And I have some of your special coffee too, hot and ready to be served.'

As Rahul and Neha sipped on the coffee made using the old woman's pink beans, and as they sipped on it silently on the spacious verandah, the walnutty aroma seeped into their heads in a slow, pleasant way. Rahul's mind was wandering around the clue, thinking of a number of things that could connect coffee and rains. Neha wasn't thinking about anything specific, though she sort of knew what Rahul was preoccupied with.

As they looked out at the hills beyond the plantation, they saw dark rain clouds moving in their direction. Where had these clouds come from so quickly? It was a majestic sight though. As they kept watching, the clouds came closer, and soon enough it was raining. The heavens poured their heart out and the coffee plantations around them were soaked in sheets of water.

Neha reached out to Rahul, tapping him lightly on his thigh. 'You said we should search for coffee that has something to do with the rain, Rahul. Here is the rain itself answering your question. Come on, let's search for coffee now. Better still, why don't we forget about the search for a while? Let's just play in the rains. You and me. It is so wonderful outside.'

He had never seen Neha in such a playful mood before. She looked more beautiful than ever, a bright glow all over her face, particularly in her eyes. Pooviah gave them raincoats and boots, and out they went, into the Cottabetta plantation, with the rain enveloping them.

The air was moist and the green leaves of the coffee plants had taken on a fresh hue with the rain washing the dust off them. The leaves seemed to be rejoicing, their thirst now quenched. Along with the plants, the tall teak trees, with the slender pepper vines climbing around them, seemed to be enjoying the rains too. An old fig tree at the entrance to the plantation appeared to be presiding over the rain-drenched symphony.

Rahul and Neha found themselves ensconced in this magic. For a spell of several minutes, there was silence. Neither of them made a sound. They just watched and listened as nature spoke to them in a lovely, refreshing voice.

Without uttering a single word, they found their hands locking into each other's. Neha turned towards Rahul and said, 'Rahul, this is the loveliest place in the world, thank you for bringing me here.'

And then she added, 'You know something, these coffee plantations are making me fall in love. With you.'

Rahul couldn't speak. He simply looked at Neha and held her in his arms. They stood in a close embrace, the soft drops of rain falling all around them in the midst of hundreds of coffee plants.

When the rain stopped a few minutes later, they were locked in a long kiss. A bird was chirping in the distance, but neither of them heard it.

Later that afternoon, when Rahul was fast asleep after a sumptuous lunch of pork curry and rice sannas, Neha wrote a few words in her diary:

Who could know that the magic of coffee,
Is not just to sip but to see?
Who could know that these moist estates,
Offer the closest, happiest, warmest dates?

Who could know that coffee can prance,
In a silent, gracious, rhythmic dance?
Who could know that this soft rainfall,
Is for my own heart a wake-up call ?

Can coffee make us love ourselves,
Struck by darts of bean-fed elves?
Or does coffee make us long for life,
In the midst of our constant daily strife?

Coffee love, do you rise like steam,
Warm aromas that make my dream?
With delicious magic by your side,
On what carpet am I astride?

Oh, stop these questions,
I don't know now.
What I will do is happily bow
To coffee magic, coffee love.

Neha was an occasional poet and always took time to carefully craft her lines. But this time, the words just tumbled out of her.

She stepped out of the bungalow. The rain had stopped, the air was cool and crisp, and the old fig tree at the entrance was looking down at her.

21

They had discovered the sheer beauty of the rain in the coffee plantations. Now, they had to unlock the third clue, which pointed to a deeper link between coffee and rain. As the monk said, 'Rain and mellow, we are gold and yellow.'

RG, who was delighted to see them back, floated across with his steaming white mug of coffee. 'What are you looking for, Rahul?'

'Coffee and rains, RG. Does rain make coffee mellow? Do you know about anything that links coffee and rainfall?'

RG sat down in the deep cane chair in one corner of the verandah and took a deep breath.

'Oh yes! I can tell you quite a few stories about coffee and rain. Coffee requires a lot of water to grow well. Actually, lots of rain, heat and humidity are the best for the bean. And I have some very interesting stories too. Now, listen to this unique story about rain and coffee, with some elephant poop thrown in.'

'During my younger days, Rahul, Neha, there was a British planter here called Trevor Smith. He was an expert on rainfall, used to measure the bloody thing every single day. Once, he walked out by himself, somewhere deep into the plantations, in the middle of heavy rains that lasted for a week, to understand how coffee plants behaved during such downpours. Was that necessary, I ask you? A few people saw him walk by nonchalantly, talking to the rains and the clouds. Yeah, he did that too, all the time. Wobbly in the head, that's what Trevor was, but a good chap nonetheless.

'Well, he got lost. Totally lost. For five days, I think, no one knew where he was. Not a word. His wife, Sarah, began crying on the third day. She cried nonstop. She wanted to go out and look for him, and I remember how we restrained her by locking the doors and windows. What was the point in one more person, and an honest lady at that, getting lost? Then, on the fifth day, Trevor came back drenched and with three tribal-looking people accompanying him, with long braided hair and rags for clothes. With them was an elephant that the tribals owned. The elephant was carrying three big bags of coffee beans, all picked during the heavy rains. Trevor wanted to see if these beans, many of which had fallen to the ground during the downpour, had any special taste. That's what he was doing for five days, getting these tribals to pick up the goddamned fallen beans in bloody pouring rain.

'Sarah was livid when she heard all this, but she was also happy that her husband was back home and eventually calmed down. Trevor paid the tribals handsomely and then went to work on these rain-fed beans. I am not sure what exactly he did, but eventually he made some of us taste this coffee. It had a strange, revolting flavour, very rough and full of smoke. No one wanted to smell it, let alone drink it. Trevor was sad and dejected that his rain and coffee experiment had failed. He dumped all those roasted, rain-fed coffee beans in an open yard. And then the interesting thing happened.

'Three days later, two elephants walked into that yard, ate up all those beans, stomped around happily and then walked away. Later, the workers found a lot of elephant dung in the neighbourhood, with lots and lots of undigested coffee beans in it. No one can eat and digest so much coffee, ha ha, not even elephants. They washed away the dung, sorted out the coffee beans, and someone then had the bright idea of tasting that coffee from the poop. Quite disgusting, if you think of it.

'But let me tell you that it turned out to be brilliant coffee, totally superb and with a unique taste. I loved it. That's why I remember it so well. Rain-picked coffee from elephant poop. We called it Trevor's rain elephant coffee. Nothing much came of it though because Trevor promptly died of pneumonia next year. Too much walking in the rain, I guess. But he had created such wonderful coffee. Now, as I am telling you this story, I can't help but think that someone out here should look at making this sort of coffee all over again. People who love coffee will adore Trevor's rain elephant coffee.'

Here, RG stopped with a wistful look in his eyes. Rahul, who was listening intently to this story, burst out, 'RG, what a story! This is simply wonderful. I've read about elephant poop coffee in Thailand. It's exotic coffee there, and expensive as hell. Wow, I never realized that rain added to the taste, or that we can make this rare stuff in India. This is super news. Someone should take this up and make Indian rain-elephant poop coffee big. Maybe Haroon, my boss——he's business-savvy——he would know the right guy to do this. Hey, but wait a minute, maybe this is the answer to our clue as well. Tell me? Were these rain-fed beans gold and yellow in colour? Was the coffee mellow?'

'No, Rahul. These beans were black and green. Jet black and dark green, I remember clearly. Far removed from gold and yellow. What do you expect of coffee beans that come out with elephant poop?'

After a moment, RG added, 'But you know, now that you ask me, I have actually seen coffee beans that are gold and pale yellow. Somewhere, a long while ago. Let me think, this should come back to me pretty soon. What a nice chat this was, Rahul. It's slowly bringing back all my wonderful, old coffee memories. What more can a lonely old ghost ask for?'

At this, Neha sat up and added her closing remarks to this conversation. 'I am relieved, actually, that this rain-fed elephant poop coffee is not gold and yellow in colour. Thanks for confirming that, RG. That's really not the kind of stuff I would like to rummage in, for treasure or for anything else.'

*

RG came back with his answer the next morning. When Rahul woke up, he saw the coffee ghost hovering before him, his big white head and black spectacles more prominent than ever. He had been waiting impatiently to say something. He spoke as soon as he saw Rahul waking up.

'Rahul, you wanted to know where you could find coffee beans that are gold and yellow in colour. I have seen beans like that in a small coastal town not too far away—a place called Mangalore on the shores of the Arabian Sea. Many years ago, I went to Mangalore to chase down an office clerk who had run away with a local woman. That's a different story for some other time; it didn't end well at all. Our agents there, they took me to visit some sheds where coffee beans were being dried. Very large spaces actually. What struck me then was that all the coffee there wasn't green or brown; it was actually pale yellow and gold. Almost looked like real gold.'

Rahul woke up immediately when he heard this. Usually, he would sit up for a few minutes, rub his eyes open and then close them again to try and meditate. If Neha was next to him, he would cuddle up to her and they would lie close together for some time, safe and soft and warm. Sometimes, he would even lapse back into the twilight zone between sleep and consciousness for a few minutes, and then wake up once again. But today, he was up with a start.

'Mangalore? How do we get there? Neha, did you hear that? We have something to work on!'

Neha had heard RG. 'I know of Mangalore, Rahul. Lots of my friends are from there. It's a beautiful coastal town with many scenic beaches. I've been to a few delicious Manglorean restaurants in Mumbai, and blogged about them too. I am excited to finally visit; I've never been there myself. Tell me, when do we start?'

'We should start today, Neha. Right away. We only have two weeks before I return to work. Haroon's already getting hyper about the Nippon film shoot. He texted me thrice yesterday saying that I have to be there at least a couple of days in advance. He began to complain that my holiday was getting too long, but I pointed out that he was the one who asked me to take this vacation in the first place.'

RG piped up. 'I can come with you to Mangalore. It's close enough and within my boundary. Would you like that? Actually, don't bother answering, I will just come along. I will join you in Mangalore though. I want to fly across the marvellous Western Ghats, high over the hills. Flying is such a beautiful prerogative of being a ghost, definitely a lot more fun than driving down in a boring car.'

Rahul and Neha, being mere living humans, had to hire a 'boring car'. Later that day, they were bouncing down the mountain roads to Mangalore. Rahul was dreaming of coffee coated in layers of yellow gold, being poured into huge bags somewhere. Neha, blogger of food and lover of seafood, was dreaming of eating the kane (lady fish) coated in rawa, a Manglorean speciality she loved. And then blogging about it! Both of them were also dreaming about the solution to the third clue. And, well, about each other.

They were in blue-blooded coffee country. They stopped en route in the small, quaint town of Madikeri for a hot cup to refresh themselves. There were coffee stores lining the narrow road on both sides. Out of sheer interest, they stepped into a store called Golden & Silver Mist Coffee. The shopkeeper, a bald, portly man dressed in a dhoti, welcomed them profusely and launched into stories about his coffees.

'I am Avinash Machaiah at your service, Sir. This is our very famous light-roasted arabica coffee, Sir. A very pleasant taste and aroma. My special light roasting; I do it in my own roaster just behind this shop. It retains so many of the natural qualities of coffee, Sir. You will find sweetness in the coffee, even the lingering smell of forest flowers. For just five hundred rupees, you can buy this pack. Will stay fresh for over two weeks, Sir.

'And here is our most expensive coffee: the civet coffee. Do you know that this coffee is eaten and excreted by our own civet cats? We have three types of civet cats in the forests of Coorg, Sir. They eat coffee berries in the wild and then excrete the seeds. We pick up these droppings and clean out the coffee beans. I have people to do just that when it is the right season. It is a most wonderful and interesting taste in the world, Sir, because these coffee beans have been coated with the intestinal juices of the wild cat.

'And let me tell you a secret about the civet coffee, Sir. Madam, you should hear me too, because this is important for both of you. I have eighteen regular customers from Germany to whom I send this coffee every month. They insist on it. One of them—I have his name here, Herr Helmut—tells me that this coffee gives him manly strength, you know what I mean. It is an aphrodisiac, he told me. I am an honest coffee merchant, Sir, so I told him that there is no proof of this, none at all. But if he thinks that the civet coffee gives him manly strength, who am I to deny that, Sir? He should know that best, don't you agree? This pack will cost you three thousand rupees, Sir, but you know now that it is worth its weight in gold. Madam, you can buy one for him if you want to.'

Rahul remembered RG's story about Trevor's rain and elephant poop coffee, and he asked the portly shop owner, 'That is quite a story, my friend. Do you also make elephant coffee, from elephant poop? It is pretty popular in Thailand.'

The shop owner said no. He actually didn't know anything about elephant coffee, but he was quick to add that it did give him an idea for the future.

'I always like listening to new ideas about coffee, Sir. Let me see how we can get our elephants to make the coffee you are describing. If coffee from civet cats gives my German customers such manly strength, imagine the strength they will get from elephant coffee, Sir. What a wonderful and glorious thought.' Here, he laughed aloud, as this idea formed fully in his mind's eye. For a moment, he imagined Herr Helmut in the midst of elephant-inspired manly action.

And then he continued, 'But there is one thing. You have to be careful with elephants in these parts. They can trample you. Not advisable at all to get in their way. Who knows, they may even be watching over their own poop.'

Rahul and Neha jointly nodded and agreed with the shop owner that this risk did indeed exist. But Rahul also suggested with a wink that perhaps it was a risk worth taking, given the significant benefits the venture was likely to yield.

Avinash Machaiah was quite taken in by their interest in coffee. 'Which way are you heading, Sir?' he asked Rahul.

'Towards Mangalore. We want to explore coffee there. Do you know anything about coffee in Mangalore?' asked Rahul.

'You are talking to absolutely the right man, Sir. My grand-uncle, Sharad Machaiah, lives in Mangalore and knows everything about coffee. Anything you want to know, he knows it all. Actually, he is a coffee processor and exporter. You should speak to Sharad Uncle when you reach there. Here, let me give you his phone number. But he can be a difficult man to catch. Always on the go, but a good man, Sir. Very helpful. You will see.'

Rahul and Neha thanked Avinash Machaiah, bought a pack of Golden Silver & Mist light-roasted arabica coffee, politely declined the civet coffee notwithstanding its unique benefits and said goodbye. As they left, the coffee merchant began making notes in his book, presumably about elephant coffee.

Rahul and Neha drank a quick cup of hot filter coffee in a small shop—it was frothy, milky, sugary and delicious as usual. Refreshed, they resumed their journey to Mangalore, the town where RG had seen yellow and gold coffee so many years ago. Did it still exist? If it did, would it actually take them one step closer to the unknown treasure the monk had left behind?

22

As they reached the coastal belt near Mangalore, they could feel the deep, humid, coastal air all around them. This was pure, silky, beach-and-mountain air, which combined the salty fullness of the sea with the clear, pristine beauty of the Western Ghats. The soil was deep red in colour. Rahul and Neha were struck by the lush green hills, tall coconut palms and dark red-coloured tiled roofed homes on both sides of the road.

RG, who had flown in from Coorg, descended smoothly into their car through one of the windows, immediately after the hills had ended and a few miles away from Mangalore. He seated himself at the back, next to Neha, and stretched his transparent white legs.

'How was your flight?' Neha asked in a matter-of-fact way.

'Oh, it was nice, Neha. Took off and landed right on time, which is rare these days given your overcrowded airports,' RG responded. 'And an interesting flight too. I ran into a few large birds along the way, black eagles mainly. Large birds of prey with very sharp talons and beaks, so one has to be careful and avoid them. But I've found that birds fear ghosts too, so it's not too difficult to stay clear, especially when both of us try to avoid each other. And then the black rain clouds. That's quite a journey, flying through thick clouds, unable to see clearly, not knowing which way to go. But that also makes the journey fun, trying to navigate in low visibility, and so here I am. A very smooth landing too.'

At precisely that point, Rahul's mobile phone rang, quite loudly. It had been silent for a long time. It was not Haroon and he could not recognize the long string of numbers that were showing on the screen. He took the call.

A distant voice spoke. Rahul recognized the accent immediately. Japanese.

'Is that Rahul?'

'Yes, it is. Who is this? And why have you called me?'

The Japanese voice ignored him and carried on in a grave tone.

'Rahul, I know you are in Mangalore today. We are watching your every move. Do not try to cheat me. I repeat: do not try to cheat me. Your boss and you think, very foolishly, that you can pass off old Japanese antiques from Mumbai as my family's sacred treasure. You are mistaken, so mistaken. Don't even think about trying that. Unless you find the real treasure and hand it over to me in fifteen days when I meet you in Mumbai, you are in big trouble, Rahul. I want our treasure, the one the monk stole from us, the one you are following his clues towards. Forget everything else, just remember one thing: I need that treasure. It belongs to my family, and you will find it for me.'

Rahul tried to interject. 'Who are you, and what is this treasure you need?'

But the Japanese voice ignored him totally and continued, 'If you don't do this, then beware, my friend. Today, you will see the first sign of the real dangers that can come your way if this does not happen. Be careful for your life, my young friend. You do not want to end up in Yanaka-reien in a hurry, do you, with your beautiful young girlfriend?'

Before Rahul could speak again, the man had disconnected the call. Rahul tried calling back, but all he heard was a Japanese voice message repeating itself, followed by what could only be described as mean and evil laughter.

He turned to Neha. 'It's that crazy Japanese guy again, Neha. This time, I think it is the other Yamamoto brother, calling all the way from Tokyo. He knows where we are and he is threatening us quite directly. Find the treasure and hand it over to him, or end up in that cemetery, that's what he said. He mentioned you too. What do we do?'

Neha was surprisingly calm. 'It's all empty talk and sword-waving, Rahul. Nothing more. What can two bald Japanese brothers do to us, in India that too? Let's just carry on. We are enjoying this adventure, aren't we?'

Neha had barely finished speaking when they saw an elephant charging towards their car. They were on a small village road, still a few miles away from Mangalore, and the large lumbering animal was running towards their vehicle. Running surprisingly fast, right in front of them.

Seated on the elephant, metal spear in hand, was a strange-looking man. Neha recognized him instantly. It was that silent, tall man who had accompanied Yamamoto during their brief encounter outside Annapoorneshwari Temple in Coimbatore.

The elephant was hurtling towards their car. Their driver, shrunken and frightened, froze in his seat, unable to move. This did not look like a relaxed animal that had just eaten or pooped out coffee beans. It looked like a beast out to wreak some real havoc.

Before they could react, the elephant had attacked their car. It butted the vehicle with its broad head and trunk, and the car shook violently. Then, it stood right before them, contemplating its next move. Rahul and Neha sat completely still, feeling really scared.

The elephant butted their car once again, and then a third time, with considerably more force. The last push ensured that the car was completely off the road; it nearly toppled over, but fortunately regained its balance. They saw the tall Japanese man, still sitting atop the animal, shaking his spear and looking directly at them.

Neha looked at Rahul. When the car had almost toppled, he had been thrown off his seat and hit his head on the dashboard. He seemed to be in pain. The driver was dumbstruck. Neha knew that she had to take control and deal with the elephant before it did any more damage. *But what could she do?* The animal and its Japanese mahout appeared hell-bent on carrying out their wrecking mission.

Suddenly, she had a crazy idea. She turned to RG. 'RG, can you fly outside and frighten the elephant? I think elephants might be scared of ghosts too, like the black eagles. I don't know for sure, but right now, we have to try something!'

RG had never dealt with elephants. Scaring humans is part of a ghost's life, and they are generally quite successful. But until that point, there was no recorded evidence of ghosts frightening elephants away.

RG, however, rose to the challenge. He tucked in his pocket watch, placed his spectacles firmly on the bridge of his fat white nose and flew out at the elephant, just as it was preparing to attack the car once again. His flight was calm and composed, and he decided to move directly into the line of the elephant's vision for maximum effect.

We will never know what the elephant actually saw, or thought it saw. What we do know is that with one mighty heave, it raised its front feet off the road and trumpeted loudly, just once. It shuddered, its feet returned to the ground, and it turned its head away. In less than half a minute, it had taken to its feet and was running away from the car, in a wild swaying motion, deep into the paddy fields.

Along the way, the elephant pooped several times, perhaps out of fear, thus unwittingly creating fertile territory for the restless coffee merchant of Madikeri, Avinash Machaiah, who had already begun his search for elephant poop with coffee beans in it. Unfortunately, Avinash would never hear of this episode, though he would eventually, many years later, go on to become a famous name in the world of exotic elephant coffee.

*

Fortunately, Rahul was not hurt, though he was rattled. The driver had regained his composure, and without a charging elephant in front of him, now put on a show of bravado. 'Sir, did you see how bravely I withstood the elephant? Without me, our car would have just toppled. I kept the balance, with my hand firmly on the steering wheel, staring at that stupid, big animal all the time. It was difficult, Sir, but I am a strong man. I hope you will recognize my bravery, Sir. Even a reasonable cash award will do.'

Neha shook her head sideways a couple of times, a peculiarity that Indians specialize in, and which can mean anything, both approval and disapproval. She said, 'We'll talk about that later. First, take us where we have to go, right away, to Mangalore. Let's get on with it.'

Then, she turned to Rahul. 'That Japanese guy did try to carry out his threat, Rahul. In a clumsy but dangerous sort of way. I don't know what these brothers are up to. Maybe they think they can frighten us into doing exactly what they want. Or maybe they want to scare us away. But this makes me even more determined to find our coffee monk's treasure. We'll get the better of them.'

Rahul looked at Neha, nodded and smiled. To tell the truth, her new-found confidence as they progressed on this coffee adventure was making her even more attractive. Confidence and beauty are such an irresistible combination. And then, of course, there was also the common love of coffee.

23

If the elephant attack episode had rattled them, there were no visible signs of it when they reached Mangalore. All they focused on was solving the third clue.

Rain and mellow, we are gold and yellow.

'Let's start by calling that coffee merchant's grand-uncle, Sharad Machaiah. If he genuinely knows everything about coffee, maybe he can help us find coffee beans that are golden and mellow,' said Rahul.

RG agreed that this was the best way ahead. They called Sharad Machaiah and Neha spoke to him.

'Sir, my friend and I are tourists with a keen interest in coffee. Your great-nephew in Madikeri—yes, Ashwin Machaiah—he told us that you are an expert on all kinds of coffee. Can you help us, Sir? We are looking for some information about golden coffee beans.'

'Welcome to Mangalore, Madam,' she heard his booming voice over the phone. 'Welcome to our little coffee town. Ashwin already told me about your arrival. You are welcome to meet me, Madam. Bring your friend along. I love people who love coffee. Come to the fish market in the area called Baikampady and ask for Sharad Machaiah.'

They found the house easily and were immediately shown into the sitting room. What they saw there amazed them. Each wall in the room was adorned with photographs of coffee beans. Red and orange coffee cherries, green dry beans, roasted brown beans—virtually every colour associated with coffee was up there.

Within this glorious mélange of colours, Rahul glanced around carefully to see if he could find a photograph of golden-yellow beans. And voila! In one corner was a photograph of large coffee beans that appeared to have a swollen look and a golden-yellow colour. A mound of golden-yellow beans, photographed with some sort of a shed in the background. They were on the right track!

In the centre of the room, on a spotted tiger skin spread out on the floor, sat a very big, very bald man. He sat cross-legged, with his eyes closed, and appeared to be meditating. For a few minutes there was no movement. They were silent, the man was silent, and RG in the background was silent too. A calendar with a picture of a coffee cup, hung on one of the walls to tell the date and month, swung a little in the breeze. The stillness persisted.

Finally, after what seemed like ages, the big, bald man opened his eyes and looked at them.

'Come, sit! Sit down, my friends. Welcome, welcome. I am sorry I made you wait, but I sit on this tiger skin for an hour each day, very silently, to say my prayers. It gives me the strength I need. This is the skin of a ferocious tiger that roamed the coffee estates of Coorg many, many years ago. Have you ever experienced sitting on a tiger skin, my friends?'

Rahul and Neha had to admit that they hadn't. Such an opportunity had not presented itself, until now. And, to tell the truth, such a desire had never occurred to them either. Sharad Machaiah began speaking. Surprisingly, he abandoned his line of inquiry about sitting on tiger skins and came to the point straightaway.

'I can help you on your quest, my friends. You want to see coffee beans that are golden-yellow in colour. I know where to find these beans. They are the speciality of Mangalore, of this entire coastal area in fact. So, you are in the right place, yes, the right place. What you are looking for is our famous monsoon Malabar coffee.'

Rahul stared at him. 'Monsoon Malabar coffee? What's that, Mr Machaiah?'

Sharad Machaiah asked them to sit on the floor with him. He had placed some mats for them, while he continued to sit on his grand tiger skin.

'Sit down, sit down. You have not heard of monsoon Malabar coffee, the most famous coffee of our land? Are you serious, my friends? What kind of coffee enthusiasts are you? Come on now, stand up. Come with me.'

He led them out of the house. They walked down a narrow, shaded road for a few minutes, without speaking a word. Sharad Machaiah was in front, occasionally rubbing his bald head. Rahul and Neha followed a few paces behind, and RG followed, invisible. Soon, they entered a large shed with a red tiled roof, which looked like a shipping warehouse. And then, just next to this shed, was a large outdoor area, vast and open, shimmering yellow and gold under the sun.

'Here you are,' said Sharad Machaiah with a flourish, 'see this yard here, all the way until there. Covered with monsoon Malabar coffee, which has brought us fame and glory. These beans look golden and, let me tell you, they are real gold. Pure gold.'

They looked closely to see that the yard was indeed covered by a carpet of very pale golden-yellow coffee beans. It was such a beautiful sight; the gold nuggets lying on the ground, thousands and thousands of beans stretching evenly on all sides.

Sharad Machaiah picked up a few beans from the ground, rubbed them between his palms and smelt them, 'Pick them up, feel the beans,' he urged Rahul and Neha.

Rahul did so immediately, and as he held the golden beans in his palm, he knew instinctively that this was really, really special coffee. He admired the pale gold colour from close quarters, then brought the beans close to his face and inhaled. A musty, chocolaty smell overtook him and spread into his body and mind, gently seducing his senses.

It was a faint, but beautiful and sensuous smell. The smell of humid afternoons interrupted by heavy showers, the smell of wet earth; a smell so different from every other coffee bean he had encountered. *How can coffee have so many wondrous aromas*, he thought to himself. This was heavenly! And these aromas would express themselves far more powerfully after these beans were roasted. No wonder the monk had led them here, to this unique coffee they hadn't known of earlier.

Sharad Machaiah watched them with a quiet smile. He could see that they were captivated. And then, as quietly as they had come, he led them back from the warehouse to his home, where he resumed his seat on the tiger skin. After that, he began narrating a story which was so gripping that Rahul and Neha forgot to drink the steaming hot coffee placed before them in steel tumblers.

*

'What you saw now, my friends, was monsoon Malabar coffee, the gold and yellow coffee you are searching for. My grandfather, God bless his generous soul, was one of the pioneers of this coffee. See his photograph up there on the wall. He killed rogue tigers and created some of the best coffees in the world.'

They looked up at an old sepia photograph of another bald man, even balder than Sharad Machaiah, with a long rifle in his hands. At his feet was a dead tiger whose skin looked remarkably like the piece on which Sharad Machaiah now sat, comfortably cross-legged.

'My great-grandfather, Appappa as we called him, used to work at a fine shipping agency called J.K. Thomson and Sons. Their ships would carry Indian coffee and spices to Europe, across the vast Arabian Sea and around the Cape of Good Hope. That was the only route those days, you know. Very long and open to the hazards of poor weather, and often pirates too. My Appappa also went on these voyages sometimes, got friendly with the ragged sailors, picked up all their terrible addictions. Yes, these addictions killed him ultimately. But, blessings of God Almighty, he saw the wonderful thing that happened to coffee beans on these long sea journeys. Something which stirred his great mind.

'And here is what happened, my friends. This is all real, I assure you, right out of my Appappa's old and tattered logbook, which I have seen myself. On one long voyage from India to Europe, which lasted more than four months I think, my Appappa befriended a Dutch sailor called Derrick. I still have a couple of old photographs somewhere. Derrick Van Buster was his full name, a handsome young white man with blond hair. I suspect the friendliness was not strictly platonic. After all, it was a long and lonely journey with only men on board, but as a rule I do not suspect my forefathers in such matters. That's just not the right thing to do, you know. Always respect your forefathers. After all, it is their genes that we carry.'

At this point, he looked up, winked, adjusted his crossed leg against the tiger skin and continued his merry narration.

'Derrick and my Appappa used to roam around the wooden ship to bide their time. Sometimes, they would spend long periods of private time in the holds below, where all the cargo was stored. Good sailors, just talking to each other and avoiding the harsh sunshine, I'm sure.' Here, he winked again, looking Rahul in the eye.

'Then, one day, a couple of weeks before they reached the shores of Europe, both of them smelt something in the hold. They sniffed, just to be sure, and the smells were there, all around them, mild but wonderful. They were puzzled. They went near the cargo, which was none of their business really. The smell, meanwhile, got better and better. They then discovered the origin of these smells: the hundreds of sacks of coffee beans being shipped from India to Europe!

'They tore through one of the sacks using a sharp knife and drew out some coffee beans. And what a marvellous sight they saw. No longer were the beans fresh green in colour. They now looked pale yellow, almost golden in colour. To their surprise, the beans had also swollen up in size, almost twice as large as normal coffee beans. This was where that beautiful, mild aroma was coming from. "How could this happen?" Derrick asked my Appappa. "I don't know," my Appappa told him, "I am not your coffee expert, darling, but let us ask our captain. He's been on these voyages hundreds of times. If anyone knows, it will be that crusty bastard!"

'So they met the captain, indeed a crusty Englishman with a rusty beard. To begin with, he took them to task and gave them a good whipping with his sharp tongue. My Appappa has faithfully documented all this because he was an honest man, you see. The captain told them that it was none of their business to tear open sacks of cargo. "We are a reputed shipping company. What would our customers think if they knew a couple of you were carrying on like this, ripping open their precious goods?" And then he became kinder, moved by their curiosity I think, and revealed a great secret to them.

'He said, "This is what happens to coffee beans when we cross the sea. They turn golden-yellow and swell up, absorbing all the moisture from the sea, and the monsoon rains and winds that have crossed our ship for over four months. That's what leads to the creation of this very special monsoon coffee. And that's good for us, fellows, because we have coffee merchants in Norway, Sweden and Denmark who love these golden-yellow swollen beans, and pay a fortune for them. They call this monsoon Malabar coffee because it is the monsoon winds and rains from our Malabar coast that transform the beans. Those merchants have told me that they had never drunk such mellow coffee anywhere else."'

Hearing the word 'mellow', Rahul sat up. That's what the monk's third clue had said. He ran over the clue in his mind.

Goddess from the sea, you welcome our coffee.
Rain and mellow, we are gold and yellow.

Something struck him at that moment, like an idea that drops into your mind from nowhere. The monk's clue contained a reference to the sea, and here he was, listening to a story about coffee crossing the sea. This could not be a coincidence. No! Not at all! Were they getting close to solving the clue?

'Then what happened? What's the connection between all this and that warehouse full of golden-yellow coffee that you just showed us?'

Sharad Machaiah was quick to respond. 'My Appappa, he was an intelligent man. He absorbed the captain's knowledge and kept it to himself. Many years later, he retired from the shipping company, a satisfied but restless man. Then, as he sat at home, this very home you are in today, contemplating what to do next, all this came back to him and he sensed a big business opportunity. A business opportunity in creating these very golden-yellow, mellow coffee beans, called monsoon Malabar, right here in Mangalore. As he thought about this, the bright idea that came to him was that why not expose coffee beans to the same monsoon winds and rains right here in Mangalore, for months together? Mangalore is on the Malabar coast. For many months each year it gets the same monsoon rains and winds as the wooden ships that crossed the sea. So, that should lead to the same swollen, golden-yellow coffee, he reasoned quite correctly. And what a wonderful idea it was! It worked so beautifully, my friends. He created a shed here in Mangalore, quite similar to the warehouse that you saw, but a lot smaller. In this first shed, he exposed the coffee beans to the monsoon winds, which came laden with humidity. In four months, the beans swelled up, turned golden-yellow and, with monsoon god Indra's blessings, my Appappa became the supreme creator of monsoon Malabar coffee. Lots and lots of monsoon Malabar coffee, more than any wooden ship could produce on a single voyage. Other locals watched this closely and followed with their own little sheds. Merchants from Europe lapped up this wondrous coffee and it made my Appappa very rich, though in his advanced years. This gave him leisure time to pursue his other passion: tiger-hunting. Look at this skin on which I sit. Just sitting on it gives me great strength because this was a terrifying man-eater, hunted down by my Appappa. See that photograph there, my friends.' He pointed at the old sepia photograph, pride shining all over his bald head.

'And now, my friends, let us not speak any more. What is all this storytelling worth without a sip of the real thing? Let us sit together and enjoy our very own monsoon Malabar coffee!'

The coffee was served in steel tumblers, piping hot, frothing at the top. Rahul and Neha took a sip each and sat back, their heads falling back almost simultaneously, like two wooden dolls conjoined by some internal spring. The coffee was so delicious that Neha immediately composed her next blog in her mind and desperately hoped that she would remember to jot it down later that night.

'Thank you, Sharad Machaiah. Truly lovely coffee this is. Monsoon Malabar. And what a wonderful story! Your Appappa was such a cool guy. I wonder whether his platonic friendship with that Dutch sailor continued. Just idle thinking, of course. I am interested in that sort of close historic comradeship, but you don't need to answer. And thank you for your time, for sharing all this with us. This is really so useful, Sir. I have just one last question.'

'What's that now?' asked Sharad Machaiah.

'Do you know of any goddess of the sea who may have welcomed this monsoon Malabar coffee?'

For the first time that morning, Sharad Machaiah was stumped. He did not know, and he said nothing. Coffee, sea voyages and tiger skins were the interesting canvas on which his thoughts wandered. Goddesses of the sea were another species altogether. They were not in his line of sight, at least not yet.

Rahul and Neha thanked him profusely and left, turning to look back one last time. They saw him there, seated with eyes closed once again, on his beloved tiger skin.

24

It was Neha who found the answer to the sea goddess question, quite unexpectedly at that. They had decided to spend another day in Mangalore, exploring the place and the nearby beaches of Ullal, hoping that the monk's third clue would unravel in this nice, small, coastal town of golden, mellow coffee.

Now, in their room in the well-appointed Ocean Pearl Hotel, with the day just about to break, Neha finished writing her blog on monsoon Malabar coffee. Rahul was still asleep. He had, after all, consumed an excellent but rather rich seafood meal the previous night, the sort that called for lots of rest. The fried ladyfish with spicy red masala had been particularly delicious. Watching Rahul wolf down the fish, Neha had decided to write a separate blog about Mangalorean cuisine. But first, she had to write about the coffee before she forgot what she had composed in her mind while speaking to Sharad Machaiah. The blog had come out quite well in the end. For a writer, that's always fulfilling, a good piece done and dusted. Her mind now began wandering idly.

In the course of this meandering, she thought about reading the clue once again. Perhaps some new fact or meaning would jump out at her. That happened quite often when she was writing and thinking, all by herself. She reached into her handbag and pulled out the old tin in which they had found the third clue at the pawnbroker's store in Coimbatore.

She opened the tin and pulled out the musty paper with the monk's writing.

Goddess from the sea, you welcome our coffee.
Rain and mellow, we are gold and yellow.

Then, she read what was scrawled on the reverse.

Every coffee bean tells a story, including my own, says the goddess.

Blank. Nothing struck her. She looked at the tin now, the old Parry's Lacto Bon Bon container, with scenes from famous fairy tales depicted on it in blue and white—the ugly duckling, the tin soldier, the little mermaid, a blue nightingale and the emperor's new clothes. She remembered a book from her childhood, her father reading out many of these fairy tales to her from a large colourful book once she was tucked into bed for the night. Those were warm and safe memories.

She tried to recall the name of the book. Soon enough it came back to her: *The Magnificent Fairy Tales of Hans Christian Andersen*. Yes, she had kept the book in her cupboard even after she entered high school, with its pages totally dog-eared by then—large, colourful pictures on every page; mesmerizing stories that had stoked her childhood imagination gently and lulled her to sleep. Then she had an epiphany. All the scenes on this tin, without exception, were from that happy old dog-eared book, from Hans Christian Andersen's fairy tales. A thought occurred to her: was there a reason why the monk had used this particular tin to store this clue? Was the tin a part of the clue as well?

Neha googled Andersen to know more about him.

Hans Christian Andersen was a Danish writer of stories, novels and poems. He is best remembered for his timeless fairy tales. His popularity across the world arises from the universal themes of his stories. His stories have inspired countless movies, ballets and plays. He died at the age of 70, in Copenhagen, in the kingdom of Denmark. An icon in his country, one of Copenhagen's widest boulevards is named after him.

Many of Andersen's fairy tales describe the lives of girls, women and princesses. The Little Mermaid, the Nightingale, the Little Match Girl, the Snow Queen and Thumbelina are examples. Andersen's own life was marked by his falling in love with many unattainable women, whom he regarded as goddesses, and many of his stories are indeed interpreted as references to these goddesses. Some of his better known disappointments in love included Jenny Lind, the famous opera singer; Sophie Orsted, the daughter of a famous physicist; and Louise Collin, the youngest daughter of his own mentor Jonas Collin.

Perhaps the most beautiful and moving renditions of Andersen's works comes not from Europe, but from the

Orient. The *World of Hans Christian Andersen* is a 1968 Japanese anime fantasy film from Toei Doga, based on Andersen's works. It depicts a young Andersen and how he discovers the inspirations he will later use for his fairy tales.

This reference to Japan intrigued Neha immediately. There was a lot of Japan popping up in her life these days; it couldn't be a coincidence. And the monk who had given them this tin was Japanese too. So, she kept digging deeper.

Hans Christian Andersen and his fairy tales have enjoyed great popularity in Japan, for many decades now. Every Japanese knows Andersen and his stories, whether they be school students, housewives or even monks in their stark monasteries. Often, he is known just by his initials, HCA. One of Japan's most-visited theme parks is Hans Christian Andersen Park in the city of Funabashi.

In fact, HCA has penetrated so deep into Japanese culture that you will see restaurants, cafés and bakeries named after Andersen. Little Mermaid Bakeries, named after Andersen's famous seaside character, started in the Hiroshima region. They offer delicious Danish pastries and are now present across the country. It is said that Japanese translations of Andersen's fairy tales are even more beautiful than the original stories themselves.

It was astonishing to Neha that a Danish author could be a household name in Japan. She reread everything to make sure she had understood correctly. Then she sat back and reflected. Andersen's stories went all the way from Denmark to Japan and became a part of popular culture there, even amongst monks! She also remembered Sharad Machaiah's stories of his Appappa and monsoon Malabar coffee, going all the way from India to some European countries and becoming part of coffee culture there. Wasn't Denmark one of the countries he had mentioned? Yes, it was. The gears started clicking together in her mind. She stood up from her chair in a state of excitement, shook Rahul hard and pulled at his feet for greater effect.

'Rahul, wake up! Get up now! Right now! There's something I need to tell you urgently. It's important. I think I've solved the monk's third clue!'

*

Rahul was half-asleep and still trying to figure out where he was. Vivid and extremely spicy memories of the seafood from last night were still flashing in his mind and, unfortunately, deep in his stomach as well. Neha was excited, coffee cup in hand, clear-eyed, eagerly and breathlessly unravelling the monk's third clue.

'Look, Rahul, at this Parry's tin that the monk put the clue in. Here it is, look at it. It's decorated with pictures from Hans Christian Andersen's fairy tales. The tin soldier, the little mermaid, the ugly duckling, they're all here. Andersen was from Denmark, but he is very popular in Japan too. Every Japanese knows his stories. Isn't that strange? Even in schools in Tokyo, films in Hiroshima, monasteries in some interior place called Funabashi, actually he is everywhere, even in street-side bakeries that the Japs eat from, and local stuff like that. Did you know that? I think it's fascinating.'

Rahul did not know that. His acquaintance with Japan was recent, but of rather novel vintage. He wondered where this muddled narrative was leading. Coming from the world of advertising, he believed that in such matters patience was a virtue, and that out of confusion often came clarity. So many meandering, endless client meetings had schooled him in this belief. So he waited and listened silently as Neha carried on.

'So, here's what I think, Rahul. I think this tin is very much part of the clue that the monk left for us. It's not just a container. Let's look at the clue again.'

Goddess from the sea, you welcome our coffee.
Rain and mellow, we are gold and yellow.

'So, we have now found the gold and yellow coffee, the monsoon Malabar beans. And we know they have a mellow taste, that this wonderful taste is created by the monsoon rains. The second part of this clue is clear then. So far, we're on the right track. But we still have the first line to deal with. What do we do?' Neha spoke without a pause and then continued in the same vein, answering her own question.

'We think, Rahul. So let's think carefully about the first line. Goddess from the sea, who welcomes our coffee. It must have a link to the second line, the monsoon Malabar beans. Otherwise, why would the two lines be part of the same clue? And then suddenly, the question occurred to me: where were these monsoon Malabar coffees greatly welcomed? Welcome is the operative word here. And remember what that guy on the tiger skin told us. I found him a little creepy, to tell you the truth, but he told a good story, didn't he? He said this special mellow coffee was welcomed in Europe, particularly in Scandinavia which is Norway, Sweden and Denmark. Now, see the connection, Rahul. One of the three countries where monsoon Malabar coffees have always been greatly welcomed is Denmark. Hans Christian Andersen is from Denmark, his fairy tales are from Denmark. He is famous in Japan, where our monk is from, and so he must have heard of him. And the tin in which he has carefully stored this clue has scenes only from Hans Christian Andersen's fairy tales, all from Denmark!'

Rahul's eyes widened now. Yes, Neha seemed to be heading somewhere with this. He sat up, his blanket still around him.

'So much of Denmark everywhere cannot be a coincidence. Our monk is leading us somewhere. So I think, in fact I am quite sure, the first part of this clue is about Denmark. Then who is the goddess from the sea, in Denmark, who could possibly welcome our monsoon Malabar coffee? For that answer, turn the tin around, Rahul, and look at this picture.'

She pointed her finger at one of the fairy tale figures on the blue and white tin. Rahul looked. And then, both of them looked at each other. Yes, they finally had the answer. It was there all this while, right in front of them, on this little, old tin. Neha had figured it out so well. Good show, detective girl!

'There you are, Rahul. The little mermaid. She is a goddess from the sea. Mermaids are divine creatures of the sea. And she sits by the seaside in the capital city of Denmark, Copenhagen, welcoming ships as they come into the harbour there. And what do some of these ships contain?' She paused for effect and then delivered her closing argument with a flourish, 'Special monsoon Malabar coffee from India which merchants in Denmark greatly treasure. So there it is. Goddess from the sea, you welcome our coffee. So clever our monk was!'

Rahul was wide awake by now. His wide eyes betrayed his excitement. He reached out without warning and kissed Neha on the cheek. A wet early morning kiss, sloppy and wide, a spontaneous warm gesture but without any mark of kissing distinction.

'Neha, darling, the monk is clever, but you are cleverer. You've got it all figured out. We've got some tickets to book right away—to Copenhagen and the little mermaid! Here we come. But first, let me clear my little brain with the best cup of coffee that this place can offer.'

They had coffee and breakfast at New Taj Mahal Café, Mangalore's iconic coffee restaurant. Neha was excited at the prospect of Copenhagen and authentic Danish pastries. Rahul was excited at coming closer to the monk's mysterious treasure. He knew that they had just ten days ahead of them to get to the treasure, before the Nippon Springlove film shoot began in Mumbai. Haroon had insisted that he be there, and rightly so, because a lot of their future fortune was tied to the success of this film.

But this would be crunch time in other ways too. The Yamamoto brothers had already told Haroon that they would be coming to Mumbai for the film shoot. There was no doubt that they would aggressively seek the return of their family treasure. Based on recent events, including the elephant attack, these crazy Japanese brothers were clearly inclined to some dangerous methods. Rahul and Neha had beaten back the elephant thanks to RG, but who knew what more they could be up to?

RG, the scourge of attacking elephants, had also come out with them. As usual, he held his coffee mug in his pale, white hand. They had never figured out how he refilled his mug, but whenever they saw it was always full of steaming coffee. Maybe ghosts had their own way with such things. Rahul had concluded that it was safer and more prudent for humans not to probe too much into the world of the dead.

'I will be flying back to my coffee plantations now, Rahul and Neha,' RG said. 'I cannot come to Denmark with you. It is completely out of my ghostly boundaries, as you can imagine. But this will be such an exciting journey for you. I wish I could have been there to see the mermaid, even feel her a little bit,' he said with a ghostly smile. 'The monk will be so happy to see that you have got this far. All because of your love of coffee! Yes, he left the discovery of his beloved treasure to just the right coffee couple. He must be smiling in his grave, the old phoney, rum-guzzling bastard.'

They raised a cheery toast to RG. Over the small steel tumblers of New Taj Mahal Café's famed filter coffee, they thanked him for being their guide and companion, and for saving them from the deadly elephant. RG was touched. After years of loneliness, their company had breathed fresh air into his afterlife.

Over that delicious coffee toast, they bid a fond farewell to RG, who then flew back to the only home he knew. Rahul and Neha continued their breakfast with two local specialities: tuppa dosa (rice pancakes roasted in ghee) and golli bhajjis (round, fried snacks made using flour, sour curd and grated coconut), served with thick green chutney, all of which complemented the filter coffee perfectly. All the time, Rahul and Neha spoke excitedly about their upcoming visit to the little mermaid in Copenhagen.

25

The Little Mermaid is one of the world's best known and most-loved statues. It sits on a rock just by the seaside on Copenhagen's Langelinie promenade. Unlike other famous statues, such as New York's Statue of Liberty or Rio de Janeiro's Christ the Redeemer, it does not tower over you. Instead, it is surprisingly small and unimposing—just 4.1 feet tall—but it is an icon of Copenhagen and Denmark, and beloved of the entire planet, drawing a large number of tourists throughout the year.

Amongst these tourists are a disproportionately large number of Japanese who have adopted the Little Mermaid as their own. What Rahul and Neha did not know is that one of these Japanese tourists, who came here around fifty years ago, was their own coffee monk. He had come there bearing a small package in his right hand. Now, many decades later, Rahul and Neha were there too, on the lookout for this same package. Hopefully it would give them the monk's final clue to the treasure that had been hidden so safely. Tucked away in Neha's rather large handbag were all the earlier clues: pieces of paper with the monk's writing on each of them, all the accompanying old pouches of coffee that came with each clue, and now the Parry's Lacto Bon Bon tin as well, with its Andersen fairy-tale pictures, all neatly wrapped together.

Rahul and Neha had arrived in Copenhagen last night. Now, they sat by the promenade licking their ice cream cones and gazing at the Little Mermaid. Neha recalled the history of the statue. She had read up on this during the long flight from India to Europe, in preparation for the final leg of their monk-inspired treasure hunt. The bronze statue had been created by the sculptor Edvard Eriksen way back in 1913, based on Hans Christian Andersen's fairy tale.

In that timeless tale, the little mermaid falls in love with a handsome prince. To marry him, she needs to become human. She then proceeds to strike a deal with a sea witch, who is extremely evil. The fairy tale then takes us on a gripping voyage through such evil and good, and the dilemma that the little mermaid faces. Though she is unable to marry the prince of her dreams, she eventually succeeds in her quest for an immortal soul because of her selflessness.

When this moving tale was staged as a ballet in Copenhagen's Royal Theatre in 1909, a wealthy man called Carl Jacobsen, who was heir to the Carlsberg beer fortune, was fascinated. He commissioned Eriksen to create a statue of the mermaid with the ballerina Ellen Price as the model. But Price, presumably a lady of high moral and prudish standards, had refused to model in the nude because that's how mermaids are depicted. Eventually, Eriksen's wife, Eline, was chosen as the model, and the famous statue was created and unveiled in August 1913.

As Neha and Rahul looked out at the little mermaid, her nudity struck them as the statue's most natural feature. She seemed to be expressing longing through every inch of her bronze being, with her languorously placed hands, beautiful small breasts and the intense, frozen sadness. Clothing would have obscured such longing, maybe even overpowered it. *Nudity expresses human vulnerability like nothing else could*, Neha thought to herself, *particularly for women. Was this true for men too?* She was not sure, and she didn't want to ask Rahul. It was an interesting topic that could wait for another day.

What she did want to ask Rahul was—given that they were here now—what was next. They had spent a day walking through the beautiful streets of Copenhagen, marvelling at the delights it offered—the city's historic city centre with cobbled pathways, the eighteenth century rococo district of Frederiksstaden and the historic Rosenborg Castle had provided them a leisurely day to gaze and reflect. Now, they must pursue what they came here for: the monk's third and final clue to the treasure. They knew that they had very little time.

So, she asked Rahul. He was looking quite composed and calm, a sign that he was thinking deeply about something. Rahul licked the last bits of his vanilla ice cream cone and spoke languidly. 'Neha, our monk has sent us on a coffee-inspired hunt. So, let's get some nice Copenhagen coffee, shall we? Maybe the coffee will make our minds spin in the right direction. That's happened to us several times already.'

They walked across to a large coffee shop that had a small roastery within it. The shop was warm and slick, and the range of coffees on offer was mind-blowing: full-bodied Ethiopian coffee, intense coffee from Bolivia, organic light-roasted arabicas from Colombia, Jamaican blue mountain coffee, Vietnamese civet coffee, coffee kombucha, fresh and fruity coffee from Kenya, and medium-bodied coffee with hints of cheese from El Salvador. The list drew Rahul into its web immediately, like a magnet draws iron, and he stood there for a few minutes, fascinated, reading up and down. Finally, Neha prodded him and said: 'Hey, coffee man, shall we ask for our drinks?'

Rahul blinked, turned to her and answered almost immediately. 'Yes, let's ask for the coffee that led us here, to Copenhagen and the little mermaid: monsoon Malabar coffee from India, the coffee that Europe has been in love with for decades. It will beat all these other varieties for sure,' he spoke confidently, with a sliver of the smile that Neha loved. It was a smile in the making, one that stopped short of becoming a full-blown smile.

The coffee shop did have monsoon Malabar coffee. In fact, it was highly recommended, particularly for connoisseurs who wanted something unique and different from the usual Colombian and African fare. Neha and Rahul carried their cups back to the promenade. It was a magical beverage, not merely mellow, but also beautifully pungent.

Rahul immediately recognized the musty aroma that must have developed naturally over the long monsoon. He remembered the story of the wooden ships sailing through the monsoon winds, with their precious cargo of coffee. And then he smiled as he thought of Sharad Machaiah's Appappa and his Derrick.

What delicious aromas they must have inhaled! The story was as precious as the coffee.

Then, he felt a chocolatey flavour popping up in his mouth. And finally, before he knew it, he also felt notes of spices and nuts, the sensual feel of pepper and areca nuts, grown with care on the lush green Malabar coast, wondrous stories that came all the way from the coastline of India.

'This is magic, Neha. Pure magic. The beans in this coffee hold more wonderful stories than any other blend I have tasted recently. No wonder the Danes out here love it. You should write about all these stories, you know.'

Neha nodded. She was already thinking about a piece, but all this talk of stories quickly brought the monk's clue back into her head. 'Rahul, let's take a look at that clue again. It spoke about stories, I think. Here's the paper.' She kept her cup to one side, peered into her handbag and pulled out the note with the third clue written on it.

Goddess from the sea, you welcome our coffee.
Rain and mellow, we are gold and yellow.

And then, on the back:

Every coffee bean tells a story, including my own, says the goddess.

'That line is trying to tell us something, Rahul. Think carefully. What is the coffee bean that our goddess, the little mermaid, owns? Did the little mermaid have anything to do with coffee at all? Let's look.'

For some time, Neha's question led them on a wild coffee chase. Sitting on the promenade in front of the little mermaid, they eagerly browsed the Internet on their smartphones, hoping to find an answer. They came up with interesting results: little mermaid bakeries in Japan, little mermaid enchanted bikinis and swimsuits in America, a little mermaid sunken ship, and, interestingly, a little mermaid rock band that appeared to have made some good music inspired by their own fairy tales. However, there was no evidence of coffee beans connected to the little mermaid.

'Let's look at the statue, Rahul. Maybe the mermaid herself will speak to us. Let's sip our monsoon Malabar coffee and hope that these cups hold some magic, like the beans that the old woman gave us, which got us started on this chase.'

They sat there, silently sipping on their coffee, an Indian masterpiece in this far-off Danish land. Rahul closed his eyes, partly to relish the coffee and partly out of fatigue. The coffee warmed his throat and the aromas rose slowly into the creaking crevices of his brain. He found a strange sense of pleasure overtaking his limbs, just like the coffee made with those pink beans.

When he opened his eyes, he was still there on the promenade with Neha next to him and the statue of the little mermaid in front of them. The mermaid was seated wistfully and longingly on her rock by the waterside. She seemed to be saying something to him. He followed her eyes, which were tilted downwards at her home, the sea. He followed her hands and saw them placed on the rock on which she had been sitting for a century. He looked at the rock, and then he looked at the rock once again. It was smooth and sloped on both sides, like a well-seasoned stone that nature had tempered carefully over time. Suddenly, with the next sip of coffee, something went off in his mind. He squeezed Neha's hand, speaking excitedly.

'Hey, Neha. Look at the rock on which the little mermaid is seated. Look at it carefully. It looks like a coffee bean, doesn't it? Yes, of course, it does. Neha, what if this rock is the goddess's own coffee bean, the bean that the monk's clue mentions? Look, look carefully, and tell me.'

Neha looked. The rock on which the mermaid sat was shaped just like a coffee bean. *Wow, wonderful. What a moment*, she thought. *Maybe Rahul is right. Maybe this is where we will find the answer. Was this a coincidence? Was this what Edvard Eriksen had planned to begin with, when he made this beautiful statue? And did he do so in discussion, perhaps, just perhaps, with our own coffee monk? Or maybe he did this because this was the waterfront which welcomed the monsoon Malabar coffee beans, and other coffees as well, into his beloved Denmark? Or was Eriksen the sculptor a great lover of coffee himself?*

Then, Neha felt a strange sensation taking over her. *Was this a larger coffee bean conspiracy that was pulling all of them in? Where would all this end? Very importantly, would it end badly or well? Or were they living some sort of dream, one from which they would wake up very soon, silently brewing their morning cup of coffee? Maybe the deep desire for morning coffee had given rise to all these outlandish dreams. Hadn't Freud written about things like this, deep ingrained desires and fantasies leading to dreams and visions? Freud had been obsessed with sex, but coffee was close enough.*

But Neha knew that this was no dream. Rahul, in the flesh, was next to her, holding her hand and patiently waiting for a reply.

'Yes, Rahul. That rock does look like a coffee bean. I agree with you totally. What a sharp observation. Let's walk a little closer and see if we can find the story that it wants to tell us. Our monk was really smart. Look at how he planned and configured this wonderful coffee chase for us.'

They walked up to the statue of the little mermaid. Up close, the rock looked like a coffee bean even more. No doubt about that at all. Neha tapped it at a couple of places to see if it was hollow, but she was wrong. The smooth surface amazed them. It was dark grey stone, smoothened over the years by the lapping of the waters and the breeze, some parts virtually resembling a shiny, wet mirror.

After a few minutes of examination, Rahul found one section of the rock with several words scrawled on it. There was nothing unusual about that because this was how visitors from across the world often left behind their messages on monuments, hopefully preserving their visits for posterity. It was not a good practice, because of the defacement, but unfortunately it was common. He looked at the words carefully. They appeared to be old inscriptions as many of the words were faint. *What if a few of these words were deliberately written by the monk many years ago? And what if these were the story that he wanted the mermaid's coffee bean to tell them?*

Most of these words were just names, scratched aimlessly and messily into the rock: Damien, Wilhelm, Henry, Anand. Some others were a little more descriptive: Donald meets Hillary,

King James the tenth, 'Big Rambo. And then there were a couple of oriental and Japanese names too: Takahara, Haruto and Aiko. This was visitors leaving behind their imprint, using the rough metal sticks and pins they had at their command. Such is the human urge to be remembered.

In one extreme corner, something interesting held Neha's attention. At first glance, it appeared to be a line drawing of a coffee bean. Yes, it certainly appeared to be a coffee bean, etched very carefully into the rock. Unlike the other scrawls, there was something artistic about the way it was presented. While the etching looked old, it also appeared quite deep, as if someone had used a sharp chisel to cut out the image of the bean well-pressed into the rock.

As Neha looked closer, the coffee bean seemed to contain some writing too. Yes, a couple of words were deeply etched inside the boundaries of the bean. She stepped closer. Two words quickly swam into her view. They were very clear, etched deep, though in extremely small font so that they could fit neatly into the coffee bean. The writing was in a sharp capital font, clear and precise, just two words in plain, simple English: LOOK WITHIN.

Neha turned to Rahul and tugged at his hand. 'Look here, Rahul. Look at what I found in this corner. Do you think this is what the monk left behind for us?'

26

Still at the promenade, fuelled by the excitement over what they had just found, and also by a second cup of hot monsoon Malabar coffee from the same café, Rahul and Neha could not help but marvel at how well the monk had crafted his clues.

'Think of this, Neha. Our monk identified a goddess so remote from his land, who welcomed a unique Indian coffee to this country. He imagined a mermaid as a goddess of sorts. Then, he chose a coffee bean-like rock on which this goddess has been sitting for decades. I wonder whether this rock's shape is deliberate or an accident. That will take another long exploration, I guess. After that, our monk came all the way to Copenhagen from his coffee estate in Coorg and etched this clue on the coffee bean-shaped rock using a professional chisel which he probably carried all the way. The clue itself is in the shape of a coffee bean. Wow, what a lovely thread!

'You remember his line in the clue. It just said: "Every coffee bean tells a story." That is true at so many levels. Every coffee bean does tell a wonderful story, you know. Just think of the fascinating story of the delicious monsoon Malabar coffee we are sipping right now. Remember Sharad Machaiah's grandfather on the wooden ship, with sacks of coffee being seasoned for months by the musty monsoon winds. And his Danish boyfriend, of course! Or the story of the jaggery-laced bellada kaapi that we drank on that hill near the source of the Kaveri. That's a story worth repeating. Or the story of the deep and dusky filter coffee we drank at Annapoorna Hotel in Coimbatore. Or the old woman's story of her magical coffee beans. A small, green bean and so many big, colourful stories.'

Neha listened, fascinated. She piped in, 'Yes, Rahul. The clues are superbly crafted. But now what?'

Rahul continued his narration, as if he had not heard her. 'Then again, it is this coffee bean-shaped stone which has this drawing etched on it. So, once again, here is a story told by a coffee bean. And finally, on the stone is a drawing of a coffee bean, with two words written inside it. So, quite literally, it is a coffee bean within a coffee bean, telling us a story through two words!'

Neha nodded, but she was now fixated on getting to the bottom of the meaning of these two words. So, this time, she firmly interrupted Rahul's flow of words.

'Yes, Rahul, every coffee bean does tell a story. The monk has brought that message home to us quite cleverly and clearly at every step in this adventure. But now, what story do these two words tell us? We have less than a week left before your much-awaited film shoot begins in Mumbai. So little time and so much to do! It's been clue after clue, that's all so far. We haven't seen even a hint of the monk's treasure yet. Let's just focus on these two words. What do you think?'

She pulled out a small card and a pen from her handbag, which was now feeling quite heavy and cluttered thanks to all the pouches of old coffee beans that had come with each clue. She wondered why she was carrying all these old pouches, but she didn't want to throw them away either.

She wrote out the two words on the card in sharp capital font. Then, she drew the rough outline of a coffee bean around the words—similar to the bean etched on the stone. Surprisingly, her drawing came out very well. *That's a nice touch*, she thought. *I must have a little bit of an artist hidden inside me somewhere.*

Rahul sipped on his coffee and stared at the card for some time. His mind wandered a little as the coffee seeped deep into his gut. Drinking coffee and staring into space did this to him always; his mind ended up wandering. He thought of the monk and tried to imagine his train of thought as he wrote those two words within a coffee bean. *Why would the monk ask them to look within? And look within, where?* They could look within a million places here, there and everywhere.

Then the other line in the clue also swam into one corner of his coffee-filled brain: 'Every coffee bean tells a story.' What if the monk had drawn the coffee bean on purpose because he wanted them to look within coffee beans? This was all about coffee, wasn't it? But where were these coffee beans? Back in the estates of Coorg?

Neha nudged him. 'Rahul, don't blank out now. We have work, solving these two words and finding the treasure.'

Rahul came out of his monsoon Malabar-induced reverie. 'These two words were on my mind, Neha. That's exactly what I was thinking about. What if our monk wants us to look within coffee beans? After all, that's what he's given us as a clue, that every coffee bean tells a story. But then, which coffee beans? And where?'

An idea formed in Neha's mind. 'Good thinking, Rahul. And here's the thing. He has used the word "within". It must mean something, Rahul. Let's look for coffee beans within us, maybe where we have been, or within what we own.'

'And where, Neha, do we have coffee beans with us? I don't own any, except those pink beans we bought from that old woman, which I think we have already consumed.'

That was quite right, thought Neha. They didn't own any coffee beans. This would require fresh thinking. She opened her handbag to drop the card and pen inside. As she did so, her hands brushed against one of the old pouches of coffee beans. It had a soft but knobbly touch. Instinctively, she pulled it out. It was a pouch that had accompanied one of the clues. She looked at it. A simple, old, greying cloth pouch tied up with a thin, knotted red-coloured thread. She looked at it again. And then she quickly stood up, holding the pouch in her right hand.

'Rahul, look here! We do own coffee beans. To be exact, three pouches of old coffee beans, left to us by our monk with each clue that came our way!'

Then she sat down equally dramatically, still clutching on to the pouch in her outstretched hand.

'Why would he leave these pouches of coffee beans with the clues, Rahul? Surely not just for effect. Maybe he wants us to look within these pouches, maybe that's what the "within" means!'

27

They decided to undertake this 'look within' activity in the secure confines of their Copenhagen hotel, to avoid any Japanese snooping. Though they had not yet seen their Japanese stalkers in this mermaid city, who knew where and how low people stoop to snoop.

They got back to their cozy room in a beautiful red brick building overlooking the waterfront. The most prominent feature there was a queen-sized bed that virtually filled up the entire space. The bed was fashioned with thick pillows and a cotton sheet with large sunflowers all over. The mattress itself was remarkably soft, comfortable in a nice, squishy sort of way, equally supportive of both frenzied movement and sound sleep, as they had happily discovered on their first night there. It may not have had the celebrated patented springs of Nippon Springlove—the film shoot for which was coming up in less than a week, Rahul remembered with some anxiety—but on the whole it had worked quite well. Now, it was about to serve another important purpose.

Neha opened the first pouch and smelt the contents. This was the pouch that they had got with the first clue, at old man

Pandian's house. It had a musty coffee bean smell with a familiar nutty aroma. *Would it send them on some fantastic mind voyage again*, she wondered. She then poured out the contents on the bed, ensuring the beans fell in an empty white space between the yellow sunflowers.

The coffee beans tumbled out of the pouch. They looked very old, but well preserved. Pale green and mild yellow in colour, there were perhaps a hundred beans in the first pouch. Looking at unroasted, green coffee beans was a reminder that an infinite world of tastes and aromas can lie dormant for years and years, confined within small little berries. It is the roaster that magically heats the bean, unlocks these aromas and splashes them generously into the hot, alluring cups of coffee that millions of people lust for every day. Rahul was a prime example of these caffeine-seeking millions, and here he was, right in front of the beans, examining them and seeking out what lay within.

He spread out the mound of beans, evening them out with his fingers. And then, just like that, in a split second, he spotted it.

'Neha, look at that, look at THAT!'

A small brass key lay amidst the spread of coffee beans. It had tumbled out of the pouch along with the beans. Now that they had seen it, the key stood out, pale brass in a small puddle of green and yellow.

Neha could not control her excitement. 'Rahul, it must be the key to the treasure! We have found it!'

She leant over impulsively and, in a burst of ill-advised enthusiasm, tried to kiss him squarely on the mouth. But since Rahul was at a distance, almost on the other side of the bed, she nearly tipped over. Moments of exuberance! We have to be careful of them.

She recovered quickly and picked up the key from amongst the beans. It was made of pale brass, with a couple of faint markings—like Japanese letters—on one side. The markings made no sense to her. In fact, the key had a commonplace design and was rather small by contemporary standards. She held it against the light for a minute, examining it closely, but found nothing else of note. She then handed it over to Rahul almost reluctantly.

They opened the other two pouches too. First was the pouch from Raghavendra's coffee stall near Talakaveri, the origin of the Kaveri. Even as they emptied this pouch, Neha said, 'What delicious jaggery coffee that was, Rahul. My mouth waters each time I think of it.'

Next was the pouch from pawnbroker Ramaswamy in Coimbatore. Neha spoke again. 'I would almost die for that south Indian filter coffee at Annapoorna Hotel, Rahul. Fresh milk, fresh coffee beans and a lovely decoction squeezed out of the beans! Can we go back there, do you think?'

Both Rahul and Neha couldn't help but wonder what new surprise would the monk have put into these two small bags? Actually, as they soon found, there was no new surprise. It was just the same walnutty aroma. Old coffee beans that tumbled out readily, quite the same in all the pouches. And from each pouch emerged a key.

Rahul kept the three keys together on the bed. They made for a pretty picture and he photographed them using his mobile phone camera. *Maybe a nice snap for Instagram on a later date, after all this stuff was behind them*, he thought.

Two of the keys looked the same, pale brass, somewhat ancient-looking, and with similar Japanese markings. Neha looked at them carefully. They were similar, but not identical. *Different characters from the Japanese script*, she thought.

The third key was entirely different. It was made of steel and was marked with the number '215'. It looked far more modern and Indian. There was a small paper tag attached to it with twine. The tag simply said, 'This one is for you. Ask Pandian.'

Rahul looked at Neha. H. Jerome Pandian, the old man with the grand moustache who had served the Japanese monk loyally for several decades. The man who had asked them to choose one pouch from many and got them rolling on this grand coffee adventure. RG had told them that this was the man who knew all the monk's secrets. No wonder they had to ask him about this key as well. That would mean a long journey once again, to the land of coffee, Coorg, and to the small town of Suntikoppa where Pandian lived.

*

But before that, Rahul had the film shoot coming up in just six days. He had to be back in Mumbai for that; Haroon would not tolerate his absence. And he had the Japanese Yamamotos to deal with; they would be there for the shoot too, insisting on getting back their family treasure.

Actually, who knew! Japanese intruders could walk into their hotel room right now, attack them with fancy samurai swords and take the keys away. After that elephant attack near Mangalore, it seemed as if anything was possible. They may have been stalking them all the way here in Copenhagen. He walked up to the door of their room and bolted it using the security lock they normally used at night.

'Neha, let's sit down for a moment and think. Why has our monk left us these three keys, two with Japanese markings and one with this note in English? And, listen, just because you could not kiss me a few minutes ago does not mean you should not do so now.'

'That's easily done, Rahul. I would love to.' With this, she walked across to him, held him by the waist and kissed him on the lips. It was a deep, lingering kiss where their lips were locked together for at least a couple of minutes. Both of them used that moment of intimacy to reflect on each other. They felt good about where they had reached. *Was this adventure about discovering Indian coffee, or searching for treasure, or was it about finding themselves or each other*, Neha wondered. At that very instant, she found herself drawn into an even tighter embrace, with Rahul's firm hands on her back. For the next hour, coffee, monks, keys and Japanese intruders were far from their minds.

Later, Rahul looked at the coffee beans scattered on the bed, many of which were now crushed.

'Let's sit down and think, Neha. Why were these keys here? What should we do with them? What treasure chests will they open, and where are these chests?'

The walnutty aroma from the crushed beans had enveloped them. These were old beans, many of which had broken down instantly under the intense, shifting weight of Rahul and Neha's bodies. This familiar, magical aroma fuelled their discussion as it found its way deep into the recesses of Rahul's mind. Suddenly, Rahul found himself thinking fluently, with complete clarity. It was as if he was cutting through all the haze, walking straight through all the twists into a strange twilight zone. It was just like when he sat down, all by himself, to write those beautiful film scripts for Nidra Hair Oil and Nippon Springlove mattresses. Those stories had come out of nowhere, like the thoughts flooding his mind now.

Rahul vividly remembered the two dusky girls who had appeared in front of him at his favourite Starbucks café in Mumbai. Then there was the graveyard conversation in Tokyo. He recalled the desire of the coffee monk, conveyed through the words of H. Jerome Pandian and RG, both of whom had known the monk well during his lifetime. There were also the Japanese stalkers and the threats from the Yamamoto brothers. And who could forget the delicious, unique Indian coffees that Neha and he had tasted and marvelled over during the past few weeks, coffees they had never known about earlier. Clearly, he had discovered those coffees only because of the monk's clues in their chase for the unknown treasure. And now, finally, there were these three keys: two of them presumably of Japanese origin, and one local-looking key with a specific message.

All these memories and many more came rushing to Rahul, rapidly, without a break. Like waves on a sea shore, one commencing even before another dissolved, the memories washed on to his mind like fresh foam. He even thought that he could hear the voice of the monk, acting as a narrator for all these memories but from afar where no one could be seen. Rahul's eyes were shut in restless bliss all this while. And then there came a moment. Maybe not a moment really, but a sharp point of inflection, where all the waves stopped, and it became very clear to him what the monk wanted them to do. There was no more ambiguity.

Clarity can often be elusive, for very long periods of time. Then, it drops, plonks itself into the centre of your mind with no forewarning, when the brain is suffused with a multitude of thoughts that are seemingly leading nowhere, and some magic suddenly weaves all of them together. And when that happens, the mind feels totally free and relieved, which is how Rahul felt in that exact moment.

'Neha, please sit right here and listen to me. I just heard the monk. Yes, I heard him myself. And here is what we should do.'

For the next hour, Rahul carefully explained to Neha what his conclusion was and why. He spoke of recent events and about the coffee monk. Neha listened to him in total silence. She found the way he moved his hands to be charming, and she loved his wide open brown eyes as he took her through his long narrative. Neither of them moved because they were totally immersed in dissecting a story which was not entirely theirs, yet it belonged to them and them alone.

Rahul concluded his monologue with one last, brief question: 'Do you agree with all this, Neha?'

Neha nodded her head, signalling her complete agreement. Rahul was right. There was sound logic in what he had said. But even if you cast away all the logic in the world, if the eventual conclusion is correct, then there needn't be any qualms at all. Rahul's conclusion felt just right.

They knew what they had to do next. The key to the monk's treasure was in their hands.

*

Meanwhile, elsewhere in Copenhagen, two Japanese men sat sipping their cappuccinos and staring pensively at their phones. They had seen Rahul and Neha go around the statue of the little mermaid, sit on the promenade drinking coffee in a relaxed way, and then disappear into their hotel room. A few hours later, they had seen the young couple rush towards the airport and board a flight to Mumbai. They had met no one in the city, picked up no parcel and done nothing to even remotely indicate that any treasure had been found. Had they missed something altogether?

When Takahira Yamamoto telephoned his two men all the way from Tokyo, asking about what exactly had happened in Copenhagen, they mumbled a few inconclusive words and put down the phone after hearing his irritable and sharp rebuke. Unlike Rahul and Neha, they did not know what to do next. So, they decided to take an evening off from their fruitless pursuit and went partying with vengeance in the pulsating nightspots of the city. It did not take them long to get intoxicated. They were found in a state of stupor the next morning by the lifeguards on Bellevue Beach in Klampenborg.

PART D

THE MONK'S TREASURE

28

The big day had finally come. All arrangements were in place for the much-awaited film shoot for Nippon Springlove mattresses. The studios at Film City in Mumbai were buzzing with activity. Director Karthik Shah was contemplating a couple of final points in his usual thoughtful manner. There was tense anticipation in the air.

An ornate bedroom, resembling one from an ancient Japanese palace, had been painstakingly replicated. The walls were wooden with light-coloured paintings depicting a few slim, petite geishas meandering their way seductively through a rock garden. One woodcut painting behind the bed showed Mount Fuji with its famous snow-clad peak. It could not get more Japanese than that.

At one end of the room, a large, shiny piece of armour hung on the wall for visual effect. This was done to make it loud and clear to the viewer that this was the castle of the shogun himself and not some commoner or randomly chosen aristocrat. There was no mistake about that. Next to the armour sat a big, brass treasure chest with oriental carvings on it.

At the other end of the room was a long black scroll with Japanese script inked on it in white, running down its length. The inspiration for the entire set had loosely come from two famous castles of Japan—Edo and Himeji—with significant local improvization from the ingenious set-makers of Mumbai.

Everything had been carefully supervised by Haroon, head of Maximum Minimum Mumbai (Triple M, for short) advertising agency. He left nothing to chance and sought perfection. He was happy that his scriptwriter, Rahul, was now back from his long holiday, even if it was with some weird stories about flying ghosts, Buddhist monks and pink coffee beans, which he had begun narrating somewhat inchoately. Haroon had listened initially, mainly to humour Rahul. But it went on and on, so he suggested that they continue over a beer after the shoot was over. Haroon was sure that all of it was mad stuff, figments of Rahul's imagination.

Such quirks come with creativity, Haroon thought to himself. *One thing is clear. Triple M needs Rahul's creative juices to flow, so I can put up with a few weird and painful stories to make this possible.*

Rahul's creative juices were indeed flowing at that very minute as he stood speaking to Karthik Shah. He finished discussing the script, featuring the shogun and his concubines, and most importantly, the patented Nippon Springlove mattress.

Karthik was happy because he had never directed a Japanese-themed film before.

'I imagined this shogun as very tall and athletic, Karthik. Always on the move, active all the time with lots of energy, be it on horseback or foot, carrying his swords and daggers lightly. That's the spirit we should capture. That's why this man needs a firm mattress to rest his fatigued body on at the end of a long, tough day. The touch of the mattress needs to refresh him instantly because he needs all his energy at night too,' Rahul said with a wink.

Karthik nodded. He liked Rahul's perspective. Both of them saw two Japanese actors entering the room—the tall shogun and the slim concubine. The shogun was wearing warrior armour of samurai origin over a knee-length brown kimono. Also, he had a strange sort of headgear on. He had brought all this with him from Japan.

The concubine was wearing a red kimono with large flowers printed all over it and a plunging neckline. Her most distinguishing feature, however, was her small and dainty face, now painted white in traditional geisha style. The only non-period part of their costumes was the familiar white and green Starbucks coffee cups that they were carrying.

Rahul saw the coffee cups, the Japanese actors and said, 'The shogun's love for coffee. Way back in Japan. That's where all this started, Karthik. The story of the shogun and his monk.'

Karthik did not know what to make of this sudden and rather muddled statement. But before he could ask, Haroon joined them, accompanied by a short, portly man clad in milk-white trousers, an equally spotless white shirt, and most impressively, white leather shoes. He had a very round face and an equally round bald head, all shaped like a perfect globe. Around his neck, he wore a thick gold chain.

'Karthik, Rahul, meet Ram Prakash, the owner of Nippon Springlove Mattress Company. He has come here all the way from Mysore to see our film shoot. Ram Prakash is amongst the most famous upcoming entrepreneurs in Mysore. A very famous man.'

Rahul wondered how someone like Ram Prakash could be 'very famous'. But then this was the man giving them lots of money for the film, so he was certainly famous as far as Haroon and Rahul were concerned, wasn't he? There may be other reasons for his fame in Mysore too. Actually, such a round face deserved to be famous in its own right. But before he could proceed on this random and useless line of thought, Ram Prakash clutched their hands and spoke excitedly.

'What a wonderful script you have written, my friends. I loved it, loved it! It will make my excellent mattress very popular. We have the best mattress in the world, my friends. Your film will take it into a million homes. Wonderful, wonderful!'

He smiled a very broad smile, one that displayed his white teeth that totally matched his trousers and shirt. Then he rubbed his hands together quickly as he imagined the sales peaking and all the money he would make.

Rahul and Karthik smiled back at him and Rahul, for good measure, added, 'Mr Ram Prakash, this film will send your sales zooming, Sir. Mattresses will fly through the roof. This is a sure-fire winner, Sir.'

Such extreme confidence pleased Ram Prakash very much, so he clutched Rahul's hands even harder while everyone else kept smiling.

Haroon decided to break this smile fest. 'We must start shooting soon. Everything is ready and we don't want the Japanese actors getting tired. Mr Ram Prakash, here is a special seat for you. Right in front, Sir. You will see all the action today.'

These were prescient words because immediately after he spoke, the action began.

29

The first scene to be shot was that of the shogun feeling the Nippon Springlove mattress and showing his delight at how firm it was. This was the director's way of paying tribute to Ram Prakash, the man whose purse strings were funding this film and who was now on the sets for a while, seated comfortably in his special ringside chair.

The Japanese actor patted his armour, touched the sword that hung by his hip and took a final sip of his Starbucks latte before proceeding to enact the scene. Haroon offered prayers and clapped the customary board.

'May this be the finest advertising film in India. Yes, the best,' he said loudly from the sidelines. 'Now, here we go. Make sure you don't leave the Starbucks cup in the frame. This is ancient Japan, my friends.'

The moment he said this and clapped the board down with an unusually heavy smash, there was some commotion. Two Japanese men burst into the room. They were holding long, shiny swords. Both the men were totally bald and wore round, gold-rimmed spectacles. They were poised in a martial sort of way, almost ready to attack.

For a moment, Karthik fancifully thought that they were samurais who had come after the beautiful Japanese actress. But Rahul recognized them immediately. It was the Yamamoto brothers: Takahira and Shinko.

'Stop everything right now. Stop this shoot,' shouted Takahira Yamamoto, raising his sword above his head. 'We have been patient, Haroon. Very patient. Now, we ask you, once and for all: where is our treasure? Where is the treasure that belongs to our beloved father and our family?'

'Yes, give us our treasure now,' shouted Shinko with equal vehemence. 'We have given you all our support. We narrated our entire story honestly to Rahul-san. We gave him the idea for this wonderful film, we told him the story of the coffee monk that set him off on his search and adventure.'

Takahira continued, 'And then we brought you the best Japanese actors for your film, all the way from Tokyo. In return, all we asked for is our family treasure. We know Rahul-san has been searching for our treasure for many, many days. It is our treasure. Give it to us! Now!'

He swung his sword about, slicing a wide and impressive arc through the air.

Karthik and the actor playing the shogun looked stunned. No one moved. There was silence for a complete minute. At that point, Ram Prakash, sipping his Starbucks coffee, stood up excitedly. 'Mr Haroon, this was not part of the script that you discussed with me. But that does not matter. This must be a new scene you have added? Very dramatic, Mr Haroon. It looks wonderful. Let's continue; I want to see what happens!'

Shinko Yamamoto turned to Ram Prakash, looked him up and down and waved the sword at him directly. 'Shut up, you idiot, and sit down now. We are discussing the most important topic of our life, not your silly film script.'

Ram Prakash had never been called an idiot before, but there's always a first time to these nasty things. Now, looking at the sharp sword in front of him, he sat down immediately.

Haroon spoke. 'Takahira Yamamoto, I told you we would discuss your treasure after the film shoot was done. You had agreed to that. So, please, let's proceed. We don't have time to lose here.'

Takahira's response was immediate. 'No more waiting, Haroon-san. We have waited and waited and waited. Our people have followed Rahul-san for so many days now. We suspect that he has our treasure. It belongs to my family; make no mistake about it. We want it now, right away. No more cheating, no more waiting, Haroon-san.'

Haroon had hoped to give the Yamamoto brothers some nice Indian antiques as consolation to carry back to Japan. A brass treasure chest of Rajasthani origin had occurred to him as a good, solid choice. He had planned to assure them that Rahul would continue to search for their family treasure if they could provide some pointers on what it was. He had told himself that this sort of spin was likely to work with the Yamamotos. But things were not looking good now.

Haroon looked at Rahul, who looked right back at him. While Rahul had spoken to him about ghosts and coffee after returning from his holiday, he hadn't mentioned any discovery of the treasure.

Takahira and Shinko moved menacingly towards Haroon and Rahul. Their swords were still raised. Suddenly, out of nowhere, a female voice spoke loudly and clearly.

'Takahira and Shinko Yamamoto, turn around and face me. I have your treasure. By the grace of the gods who keep watch over Yanaka-reien, your treasure is safe, my friends.'

The Yamamoto brothers turned to face the voice. Everyone else in the room turned too.

There, clad in a beautiful, lightly patterned, blue and yellow kimono, stood Neha. Her lips were bright red like a senior geisha's and there were big white flowers in her hair. She seemed to have entered unnoticed. In her hands was a brass box that looked like a small treasure chest. Neha, the food blogger from Mumbai and, more recently, coffee lover from Coorg and Copenhagen, had just made the most dramatic entrance of her life.

Takahira Yamamoto looked at her. His expression was stern. 'We know you well, Madam. You had come to Yanaka-reien with your boyfriend, Rahul. What is it that you have for us? Let me see.'

He walked across to her and looked at the brass box closely. 'You are wearing a very authentic Japanese costume, that I will admit, Madam. But no, this small brass chest is not our treasure. I can see. This is just an old box you have bought from an antique shop. Don't try to pass this off as our treasure. I already warned

Haroon-san that we will not tolerate such cheats,' he said and waved his sword again, rather abruptly and violently this time.

Neha lifted her eyes, like a dainty Japanese maiden would, and responded softly: 'Yamamoto-san, it's not the box. That's not what I meant. But within this small box is what you seek.'

With her right hand, she slowly lifted the lid.

Haroon and Shinko Yamamoto moved closer to see what was inside. Karthik, overcome by curiosity, left his camera and wedged closer. This was turning out to be a very different film shoot for sure.

Ram Prakash, not knowing what to make of all these recent dramatic developments, also moved towards Neha but kept a safe distance from the Yamamotos and their swords. Manufacturing mattresses with patented Japanese springs was difficult enough. He had no desire to get embroiled with Japanese swordsmen now.

And then, in the midst of all this turmoil, who was this Indian woman in Japanese clothes, holding a brass box? A lurking suspicion entered and laid its ratty seed in his mind. He wished he had not commissioned an agency of madmen with links to Japanese gangsters to make a film for his beloved mattresses.

Meanwhile, Neha had lifted up the lid. The inside of the box was covered with soft, red velvet on which sat two small brass keys.

Takahira Yamamoto peered into the box and stared at the keys. He saw the faint Japanese characters marked on them. He picked up one key, turned it over in his hand and read the faint markings. Then he picked up the other one and read the markings on that too.

He repeated this process a couple of times. Everyone at close quarters could see the glint in his eyes behind the rimmed lenses. Then he called out to Shinko. Both brothers peered at the keys closely, taking an unduly long time.

Eventually, Takahira spoke. He held his bald head high and lowered his sword. His voice reflected both joy and immense relief.

'Rahul-san and Neha-san, we thank you with all our heart. Here I declare today, these are indeed the keys to our family treasure. From the markings on these keys, my brother and I have understood exactly where the treasure is stored, securely locked in Tokyo. We have been searching for this treasure high and low our entire lifetime. We thought you would cheat us, because cheating others for self-benefit is the curse of our times. So, we stalked you and warned you. But you have been truthful. We are grateful to you for having found our treasure and returning it to us. We have valuable gifts for both of you and Haroon-san too.'

It was a climactic moment, and so Rahul felt compelled to respond.

'Neha and I are grateful to you, Takahira-san and Shinko-san, for having gifted us the finest coffee adventure we could have ever imagined. And yes, I am grateful to you for the story of the shogun, which gave me the idea for this script. Those are greater than any gift that you will give us now.'

After a brief pause, he added, 'But yes, of course, we welcome your gifts too.'

As a final afterthought, a gesture towards his boss, he added, 'I have no doubt that Haroon-san is also grateful to you for your story, which gave us the idea for this film.'

Haroon nodded vigorously. This was reaching somewhere good after all. What had happened was puzzling, and he had no idea where those blasted keys had come from, or why this beautiful girl had burst into their set, dressed like a geisha. But the Yamamotos appeared to be happy, which was good news, and right now, shooting the film was his priority. The rest of the story could wait until he sat down for a beer with Rahul. *After all*, Haroon reminded himself, *he was the head of an advertising agency, not a company that searched for secret treasure.*

'Let's get on with the film, now,' he announced in a business-like fashion. 'All this was not part of the script, mind you. It just happened. This is Film City after all, anything can happen here. So move on, move on. Let's get back to the shogun on his mattress. Karthik, shall we get started again?'

Rahul and Neha looked at each other and smiled. The conclusion they had reached in their Copenhagen hotel room had been right. Their plan had worked well, and with a nice touch of drama that too. The only difficulty had been finding the right kimono for Neha in Mumbai, but a young Japanese lady they knew indirectly had been generous enough to lend hers.

Rahul put his right hand into the pocket of his trousers, felt the third key which they had found and wondered where this would lead. *That blasted coffee monk was controlling their lives*. Neha had exactly the same thought.

30

A week later, Rahul and Neha met at Starbucks, across the road from Horniman Circle. This café sometimes offered limited editions of the most exquisite coffees that no one had heard of. And now, there was also seasonal baked mango yogurt on the dessert menu.

Rahul ordered an India Estates Blend coffee and persuaded Neha to order the same.

'You should try this, Neha. This special coffee comes all the way from Coorg, which we know so well now. Do you remember our time through the lush green coffee plantations there, with RG floating behind us? This coffee will remind you of the plantations for sure. It has beautiful herbal notes, with hints of citrus and a chocolatey mouthfeel. Listen, Neha, I have tasted this coffee before, and I could almost taste Coorg in my cup. A medium-roasted arabica is what you will get.'

'Stop showing off your coffee knowledge all the time, you idiot. But yes, I'll go with an India Estates Blend too. Let's see what it holds for us.'

They sat silently until their coffee arrived in huge porcelain mugs. It had an intense sweet aroma and a bold flavour with notes of citrus. Neha thought that she could also sense chocolate and cinnamon, and that was when the coffee teased her tongue with more complex tastes which she could not put her finger on. The coffee sent shivers of satisfaction down their spines.

'Rahul, I wish we had those pink beans with us again, the coffee that took us all the way to Japan. Was that magic, I mean, what really happened to us then?'

'I wish I knew, Neha. Maybe we will never know. That's why magic is magic, because you can never fully understand it. Sometimes, we should not try to pierce the magic veil. All our lives desperately need some magic from time to time. But I think we were finally right, you know. Those two keys belonged to the Yamamoto brothers and our coffee monk wanted us to find the keys and hand them over to the rightful owners. That's why he had sent us to Japan in the first place to meet them. That's why he left a label attached to only the third key, telling us that this specific key alone was for us. This implies, as we rightly surmised, that the first two keys were not for us. They had to be handed over to the Yamamotos. I wonder what treasures those keys will unlock back in Japan!'

He continued. 'But you know what I think, Neha? Those pink beans that took us to Japan must have been stolen from the monk's plantation by that wrinkled old lady. We experienced the pure magic of his special coffee and it took us where he wanted us to go.'

Neha reached out and held Rahul's hand. 'This India Estates blend is taking me places, Rahul. It is so beautiful. Superb recommendation by the only coffee grandmaster I know. Did I tell you, I am getting to really like him?'

And before he knew it, she switched the topic abruptly. 'Hey, listen, have you brought the third key with you? What do we do now?'

Rahul took out the key from his pocket, as if on cue, and handed it to Neha. She looked at the paper tag attached to it. It was a musty old card with faint, but very clear, writing.

This one is for you. Ask Pandian.

'We go where the key wants us to go, Neha. We can't leave our adventure unfinished, can we?'

*

Rahul and Neha went to H. Jerome Pandian, loyal housekeeper to the monk and keeper of his secrets. They arrived at Pandian's house in Suntikoppa to a very warm welcome.

'Ayya, Amma, sit down, sit down. Always coffee first and talking later.'

He served them filter coffee in small steel tumblers, just like he had done on their first trip several weeks ago. The south Indian kaapi, rich with milk and sugar, with froth at the top, had a golden glow. Neha sipped a little, and after their long drive, it felt like the nectar of heaven on the tip of her tongue.

'Ayya, Amma, I made this coffee for you from the new season's coffee crop that has just come in. These are washed robusta beans from my master's plantation, Edobetta. Roasted by me, right here in my home, on my own iron pan. I learnt the secrets of roasting from my master, God bless his soul.'

Pandian was in an expansive mood that morning. As they sipped their coffee, he spoke about his roasting technique.

'Ayya, the beans change colour from green to yellow to golden brown on my iron pan. All this while, I need to constantly adjust the flame. My master taught me how exactly the flame should behave. Then, suddenly, I hear the first crack, and soon I have to lower the flame. After a few minutes comes the second crack; the beans are dark brown. Ready to brew, ready to serve! The secret lies in the heat, the stirring of the pan at the right time. Would you like to see?'

Rahul was tempted to say yes because he wanted to roast his own beans too. That would be wonderful; it would take his coffee involvement a few notches higher. But they were here on a mission and they had to get back to Mumbai within a couple of days.

'Thank you, Pandian. Sometime later; not now. You know, we are here just to ask you a question.'

'Ayya, my master had told me to expect you back with a question. And he had said that I should also brief my son, just in case I wasn't alive when you returned. I am now ninety-eight, Ayya. See my hair and my skin. I don't know how much longer I will live. But God, and my master, gave me a very good life. And this wonderful moustache. I am happy. Ask me, Ayya, ask me.'

Rahul reached into his pocket and produced the third key, the one with the number '215' marked on it, and the small card that said: 'This one is for you. Ask Pandian.'

'Pandian, do you know anything about this key? We found it in one of the pouches of coffee beans that your master, the monk, left for us.'

Pandian looked at the key carefully. Then he asked Rahul to hand it over. He cupped it in his hands, closed his eyes and turned towards the heavens. For a few minutes, there was no movement. He appeared to be praying. Then, he opened his eyes and spoke, 'Ayya, Amma, I am so happy to see this key again. I know it very well. I used to accompany my master when he used this key. Now, he has left it to you. He wants me to take you to the place where it will work. And I will take you there, right now. But first, finish your coffee, and I have some more left in my filter to serve you.'

They finished their coffee and got into their car, accompanied by Pandian. Pandian directed the driver. Neha's face betrayed excitement. This was the culmination of such an interesting chase. They were finally close to the treasure that the monk had decided to leave for them.

When they reached, they realized that it was the local branch of a large bank. Pandian took them to the person manning the lockers at the branch. They displayed their key, Pandian affixed his thumb print and they went into the strongroom. A bank official followed them with his own master key.

Inside the strongroom, they stood in anticipation as the bank official found locker number 215. It was at the bottom. The official first used his master key and then asked Rahul to insert his key. The key glided in smoothly; there was a quick twist and the locker opened.

There was a large, sealed manila envelope inside. Neha was overcome with impatience, so she dived in and extracted the envelope. Rahul and Pandian stood by her side.

On top of the envelope was a single line, written in the monk's handwriting.

For you who love coffee so much.

Here is the treasure I leave for you. I hope you will accept it.

Slowly, now with trembling hands, Neha looked at the envelope, turned it up and down, and finally handed it to Rahul. Pandian felt the tension in the air, so he stepped back gently, twirled his grand moustache and said, 'Ayya, Amma, this is my master's gift to you. Take it with you. May my master's blessings be with you forever.'

31

They opened the envelope seated on the verandah of Cottabetta Bungalow. Unknown to them, RG was there too. He was perched invisibly on a chair nearby, with his steaming cup in his hands. The sun was setting on the coffee plantations. Dense greenery dropped down on the mountains all around them. A few birds twittered, anxious to reach home quickly before nightfall. Pooviah had just served them hot coffee with banana chips on the side.

Inside the envelope, Neha found a sheaf of documents held together by a large clip. On top of it all, she found a letter written by hand on a ruled paper, in turquoise-blue ink.

She wedged closer to Rahul on the cane sofa and began reading aloud.

My dear fellow coffee lovers,

I do not know who you are, but I know that you love coffee dearly because you have reached so far. How could you have solved my coffee puzzles, my friends, unless you were so steeped in the magic of this beloved drink? Thank you for indulging me by following the clues I left for you. You have done well and I want you to know that my secret treasure can now be yours. Not yet, though. I may be dead and gone, but please indulge me one more time, my friends.

Let me tell you my story first. I am Asahi Saito, a monk from the city of Osaka. 'Saito' means an image of purity and divine worship, and my order required me to be pure in search of the divine. I was engaged in prayers all the time in Japan. Then, one day, I met Shogun Yoshinobu who had retired from active life. He liked me and got talking to me, and then he introduced me to something that changed my life. He gave me my first sip of coffee.

It was magical. I remember drinking from that cup in Yoshinobu's home and was convinced that it was divine nectar in my hands! Yoshinobu shared my excitement because he had obtained this coffee only a few days earlier from the land you now call Turkey. He was, in fact, the very first man to bring coffee to Japan.

For the next many months, we sampled a hundred different varieties of coffee from many parts of the world. Yoshinobu was very well-connected and many couriers brought him coffee beans, which he carefully roasted and brewed using a method that he alone knew. He taught me that method too and we shared our views about the merits of each coffee. Oh yes, he took great pleasure and pride in all his coffees.

Yoshinobu had hosted foreign delegates with special coffees too. One of those coffees, he told me, was totally magical. He said this particular coffee made people live out their dreams. Sometimes they went crazy when they drank this, he told me, and sometimes they became wise. But they always liberated their minds and became what they wanted to be. He said this coffee came from a secret source and was marked by pink beans. He wanted me to preserve this secret for the future. He gave me a box of these fresh coffee seeds, which he had obtained from somewhere, and asked me to plant them and nurture them. I promised him that I would do that.

Initially, I planted these seeds in my yard in Japan and a few coffee plants grew there. Yoshinobu was right. The coffee from these plants was magnificent and magical. Once, when I drank it, my mind was transported to India, the land of the Taj Mahal, the monument of love which I had always wanted to see. So, after Yoshinobu passed away, I decided to travel to India. I spent two months here and fell in love with the country, one with beautiful, happy, talkative people. Not a wealthy country, but indeed a rich land. I also discovered that coffee was grown in the southern part of India. So, I decided that I would fulfil my promise to Yoshinobu by moving to India forever and living here as a planter of coffee.

That is how I established the Edobetta plantation, which was the love of my life. I bought land in Coorg and, at the very beginning, I planted the special pink coffee seeds, which I got from the plants in my own yard. Then, I planted other well-known varieties of Indian coffee too. The life of a planter was destined for me. I loved this life, the greenery all around, the fresh outdoors and the elephants and flying squirrels.

I cultivated Edobetta with all my heart: it became part and parcel of this beautiful coffee-growing land.

I gradually fell head over heels in love with Indian coffee. What amazing variety of coffees this country has, which the whole world should discover someday. My favourite was always filter kaapi with milk and sugar. And then coffee with jaggery: they call it bellada kaapi. Then there were washed robustas; monsooned Malabar coffee; Mysore nuggets; arabicas of the Shevaroys and Manjarabad; and so many more. All treasures of this fertile land.

But in the midst of this, I had not forgotten Yoshinobu and Japan. Before he died, Yoshinobu had left with me two keys to a treasure, which he wanted to share with the sons of his good friend Yamamoto. I assured him that I would do that. I brought those keys with me to India and decided to hand them over to the Yamamotos when I next visited Japan. I visited Japan a few times to be sure, but unfortunately I could never locate them. So, the keys stayed with me. My friends, I'm sure you now know which keys I am referring to.

Meanwhile, in India, I also made many friends. There is my loyal bearer, H. Jerome Pandian, who served me for over fifty years. He is the best human being I have ever known. Then there are the planters too, including that great, big man Scott Ramsey, with whom I spent many enjoyable evenings. We began growing old together, all of us, enjoying the good times. Occasionally, I would visit a monastery nearby to wash away my sins.

Edobetta plantation remained my first love. As I turned older, I wondered who would run Edobetta when I was gone. One thing was clear to me: Edobetta had always been a labour of love. So, it would have to be a person who loved coffee because Edobetta was all about deep love for coffee. With some further thinking, I decided it would have to be a couple, not just one person—because they could then live here forever with each other, looking after all the coffee with care and love. Not everyone can be a single monk like me, you know.

That is when I devised this game which you have played so well, my friends. Of course, with some help from my good friend Scott Ramsey, who had by then died of hard drinking and become a ghost in these parts, even when I was alive. Ah, the coffee ghost! He assured me that he would continue to haunt this area in a friendly way and help locate extreme lovers of coffee, who in his judgement could inherit my dear old Edobetta. And my little game, with all its clues, would of course test how much these people actually nurtured a love for Indian coffee.

I also thought to myself, with luck and some of the magic from my pink coffee, that these people could help me hand over those two keys to the Yamamotos. I decided to take a chance with this. So, my game plan took all this into account. I do not know if you managed to find the Yamamotos and hand over their keys, but if you did, please accept my heartfelt thanks. Shogun Yoshinobu will be very happy.

The rest is now before you, my friends. Look at the bundle of papers in your hands. These are the property papers to the

Edobetta estate. You will find all the relevant documents and land deeds here. You can have this coffee plantation forever, if you wish to. This is my treasure, the only treasure that I owned.

There is only one condition though. You will have to live in Edobetta for the rest of your life and take care of this estate, like your own child. Think about this carefully. If you accept this condition, you can have my coffee plantation. But if you don't accept this, then I would prefer that the plantation be donated to a local charity who will take good care of it. I have mentioned the name of this charity within these papers.

I hope you will accept my treasure. Many years ago, my life opened up to coffee. It has been the most delightful voyage, living with the coffee bean and enjoying its unrivalled pleasures every single day. Like me, you are great lovers of coffee. May this treasure open up a new coffee adventure for you too.

I remain, forever,

Asahi Saito.

*

Neha looked up from the monk's letter and felt Rahul's gaze on her. Their eyes locked together.

This was an unexpected gateway to an exciting, seductive, new life. Waking up with coffee, dancing with its blossoms, trekking in its trails, inhaling its aromas, luxuriating in its flavours, nurturing its fruits, travelling the world to discover new coffees,

238

creating new blends for the world to savour, drowning in its infinite varieties and bringing to life the glories of Indian coffee. Imagine doing this every single day.

When she looked at Rahul again, she thought she could see a new light in his eyes. One factor was surely their love for coffee, which had grown during the past few weeks. And a life with each other, forever? She could never be sure, but it appeared to be a nice prospect.

But then, there was their life back in Mumbai—food blogging, advertising films, friends, shiny lights and the throbbing pace of one of India's largest cities. Fame and fortune, in the city of dreams. Oh, and not to forget, Haroon and Starbucks. The familiar, secure life they knew and had settled into so well.

How extreme was their love for coffee? Neha knew they would have to answer this question soon. Even as she thought about this, Rahul turned to her and asked, 'A tough choice, Neha. But I have a suggestion. Shall we consult RG?'

From his invisible perch, RG adjusted his spectacles, remembered the monk and smiled.

Rahul continued. 'But I think that can wait for a while, Neha. For now, let's just walk outside. It's so beautiful here and the orange skies have lit up the evening.'

So, they locked that question deep in their minds and walked out of the verandah at Cottabetta Bungalow, hand in hand—Cottabetta, the cold mountain that looks out over an infinite carpet of coffee plantations in Coorg, home to magnificent coffees that warm up the world every single day.

In the distance, they heard the charr-charr of a woodpecker. They knew that it was speaking to them. They only wished that they could make out what it was saying.

*

AFTERWORD

This story has its roots in my long-time love for coffee and a somewhat recent fascination for storytelling and magic realism. Rahul and Neha took shape in my coffee cup, as did the friendly ghost, RG. I loved the thought of including a nice, helpful coffee ghost in this adventure, though I do not know of any ghost that lives on coffee plantations. If you do go on your own coffee adventure, and perchance find a ghost, do let me know.

You could begin your coffee adventure at Cottabetta Bungalow, where Rahul and Neha stayed, or at one of the equally beautiful heritage bungalows tucked deep inside the lush-green coffee plantations of Coorg in south India. Here, you can savour the best that Indian coffee offers, beginning your day with a heavenly cup made from the local arabica and robusta beans that are grown and nurtured with love, by farmers who have made coffee their home.

I have enjoyed staying at Cottabetta Bungalow several times. Each time I have returned refreshed and rejuvenated thanks to the aromas of fresh coffee, the chirping of the great black woodpecker, treks through the coffee plants and the delicious Kodava curries. A good place to begin, if you are planning such an adventure for yourself, is Ama Plantation trails (amaplantationtrails.com), where you can discover many of these quaint bungalows and plan your own coffee plantation holiday.

Indian coffee is beautiful and unique. It is already popular in many parts of the world and deserves to be discovered by every coffee lover worldwide. My favourite Indian coffee is the monsoon Malabar coffee, one of the heroes of this story. It is musty with the smell of the rains, pungent with notes of pepper and spice; and its mellow aromas envelop your mind completely. I also love the one-by-two filter coffees of my home town, Bangalore. My favourite coffee spot in India is a small, cozy corner at the lovely Starbucks store in Horniman Circle, Mumbai, where this adventure evolves.

Since this book has been inspired by coffee, I would like some of its proceeds to go back to the coffee community. So, I have committed to donate my author's royalties from the first edition of this book to the Coorg Foundation, which has been established by Tata Coffee, to promote and secure the upliftment, well-being and welfare of the local community of Coorg, the proud home of Indian coffee. One of the notable projects of this foundation is Swastha, which educates, trains and rehabilitates differently abled children from the region. Your purchase of this book will therefore also help a child in the coffee community. Thank you very much.

Each of us has a full lifetime to experience the magic of coffee. I hope you discover your own special coffees. I would be delighted to hear about them at bhatharish@hotmail.com.

ACKNOWLEDGEMENTS

I would like to express my sincere thanks to the following people and institutions that made this book possible.

To Milee Ashwarya and the team at Penguin Random House India, for their belief in this book. Without that, the story would have been stillborn. Milee, thank you for your friendship and support.

To my editor, Saksham Garg, for brilliantly shaping this book. He not just edited the story but also enriched it by adding many superb and unexpected touches along the way. His insightful efforts helped shape both plot and characters, and many of his editing interventions were as magical as the coffee itself.

To my copy editor, Aslesha Kadian, for her meticulous work on the text. Her excellent command over the English language and her instinctive feel for the right turn of phrase have gone towards tightening the story and making it so much more relaxed and enjoyable.

To Sreelakshmi Hariharan, Theresa Sequeira and Arlene D'Souza, my colleagues at the Tata Group, who have helped me in many different ways during the writing of this book.

Acknowledgements

To the Tata Group, where I have worked for more than three decades now, for encouraging my love of writing. This is my third book, and all three have been possible only because the Tata Group has provided me space and support to discover my passion for the written word, alongside my day job as a marketer and manager.

To my mother, Jayanthi, for her blessings. She has known for some time now that I have been writing a story about coffee. We have had occasional conversations about the progress of the tale, and I now look forward to gifting the book to her.

To my daughter, Gayatri, who has been a source of constant support in all my writing endeavours. If ever there is an epilogue to this story, she would be best placed to write it because her spontaneous, irreverent epilogue to my previous book (*The Curious Marketer*) was an instant hit with all readers.

And finally, to my wife, Veena. She is the love of my life and I thank her from the bottom of my heart for her strong support throughout the writing of this book. She is the first person to have read this story, every bit of it, and her critical observations and suggestions have helped shape many parts of it. She even took me away on writing holidays to the hills near Mumbai to ensure that I had the required time and space to think, develop and write this book. What would I do without you, Veena!

A NOTE ON THE AUTHOR

Harish Bhat is an author, columnist and marketer. He works with the Tata Group, where he began his career over thirty years ago.

His first book, *Tata Log*, was a bestseller and continues to enthrall readers with stories from the modern history of Tata. His second book, *The Curious Marketer*, addresses the topic of why and how curiosity is so important for marketers, and, indeed, for everyone. He also writes popular columns for *The Hindu BusinessLine* and *Mint*.

By day, Harish is brand custodian at Tata Sons and serves as a director on the boards of many Tata companies. Previously, he was managing director of Tata Global Beverages and chief operating officer of the jewellery and watches businesses of Titan Company Limited. An avid marketer, he has helped create many successful Tata brands.

An alumnus of BITS Pilani and the Indian Institute of Management Ahmedabad, he has won the IIMA Gold Medal for scholastic excellence, and later the British Chevening Scholarship for young managers. In 2017, BITS Pilani conferred on him its Distinguished Alumnus award.

Harish is an incorrigible foodie and fitness freak. He relishes the written word and loves spinning a good story. His wife, Veena, is a data scientist. They have a college-going daughter, Gayatri. Harish and Veena live in Mumbai, where he loves gazing out at the distant sea over his cup of freshly brewed black coffee. He can be reached at bhatharish@hotmail.com.